MENDING BROKEN ROADS
(*Edenton Bay Romance* Series, Book 1)

Elizabeth Woodrow

Cover design by Vila Design

Published by Van Rye Publishing, LLC
Ann Arbor, MI
www.vanryepublishing.com

ISBN: 978-1-7340344-6-2 (paperback)
ISBN: 978-1-7340344-7-9 (ebook)
Library of Congress Control Number: 2021948019

Dedication

For my parents. You always believed I could do it.

For Samara. My reason for everything.

Contents

Chapter 1

Callie St. Claire

As I loaded up my Jeep with all my worldly possessions to leave the prison I called Indianapolis, Indiana, I knew my destination but had no clue what lay ahead. I had wanted to leave this place ever since my parents died fourteen years ago, but I was sixteen and forced to live with my Aunt Carla. She was a cruel woman. She made Cinderella's stepmother appear to be a saint. The minute I turned eighteen, Aunt Carla kicked me out with nothing but the clothes on my back and a few possessions. I'm not sure why I didn't leave Indianapolis then. Was it my fear of the unknown? Was it my lack of money? Probably a mixture of both.

My aunt had taken everything my parents left me except the yellow Jeep. They had given it to me just before I turned sixteen. It was right before they left for their trip from which they would never return. However, on my twenty-first birthday, I received a letter from my parents' attorney stating they had left me a trust I could start receiving on my twenty-fifth birthday. And I did. Even with the money, though, I still couldn't bring myself to leave Indianapolis. It was my only connection to my parents.

After turning twenty-nine, I decided to face all my fears. It was time to break free from the chains of grief that bound me to the past. I needed to step out of the past, not even into my future but into my present. I wanted to be happy and feel free, and I couldn't do that in Indianapolis. The bad memories outweighed the good. So, I laid out a map, and I prayed for God to show me where He wanted me to go. I closed my eyes and planted my finger on the map. I opened my eyes and glanced down at my finger. Edenton, North Carolina. Never heard of it. But I was excited and nervous and everything in between.

I was nervous because I was about to embark on a solitary journey to a new place. New places didn't fare well for fat girls like me . . . or maybe it was the other way around. I had struggled with my weight my entire life and had been on every diet known to man with nothing but utter failure. Meeting new people was a struggle because, well, people were just plain mean. Each new school year or job brought about new torment with new bullies. Not to mention the years of abuse I endured at the hands of my aunt. Would the people of Edenton be any different?

I was excited because, after doing some research on the town of Edenton, I found it might be the perfect place for me. Boasting a population of about 4,700 people, the small town was just off a body of water called Edenton Bay. The pictures of the quaint shops on the main strip of road and of the historic Victorian and Tudor houses amazed me and drew me in. Even though I had spent my entire existence in a large city, I always thought of myself as a small-town girl.

With my hair in a frumpy bun and dressed in sweatpants and a T-shirt, I took one last glance around before getting in my Jeep. I breathed deeply, started the engine, and with hope flooding me, I drove away. It was the beginning of June. Summer was just kicking off, so the humidity in the air was almost nonexistent. I could hear the birds chirping as the hustle and bustle of the city hadn't been awakened fully yet. The morning was beautiful and full of promise. Relief, excitement, and fear were fighting for space inside me. They were doing their best to tie my lungs into a pretzel. I thought about my life and what I was leaving behind. I hoped the minute I drove out of the city, the nightmares would be locked away forever.

As I traveled down the highway, there wasn't much to see other than some greenery, truckers, rest areas, and the occasional gas station or fast-food restaurant at an exit. After six hours of the non-picturesque highway, I stopped to get gas, get something to eat, and use the restroom. I was somewhere in Nowhere, West Virginia. As I slid from the driver's seat, my legs wobbled like Jell-O. I jiggled them so I could stand firmly on the ground. I used the ladies' room and grabbed a snack of Nacho Cheese Doritos, a small sandwich, and a bottle of Diet Dr. Pepper. After I paid, I traipsed back out to the pump where I had left my Jeep. I filled the tank before getting back on the highway.

Before I knew it, after almost twelve hours of highway hypnosis, I was traveling on US-17 N into Edenton. I stared out the window at the beautifully landscaped, green lawns as the smell of fresh-cut grass infiltrated the vents of my Jeep. I inhaled deeply—it was one of my favorite scents. Once in Edenton, I drove down Broad Street and became enchanted with the lavish, old, Victorian homes I passed along the way. A sense of home drifted over me—something I hadn't experienced since my parents died. There wasn't any one thing I saw that caused this feeling; it was just something that resonated throughout my entire being.

I made my way to the Edenton Inn, the place I would be calling home for a while. As I pulled up, I gasped at the sight of the old, red-brick, Victorian with a wrap-around porch—my favorite. Stepping out of my Jeep, I glanced around to survey the area. It was just after 9 p.m. A few kids rode their bikes along the sidewalk. Were they racing to get home before the streetlights came on? Fond memories floated into my mind. My friends and I, before we were teenagers, would leave where we were with just enough time for each of us to sprint into our houses right before the glow of the streetlights filled the darkening sky. The sun set low on the horizon, casting hues of pink and blue across the sky. It would be dark soon. The inn was surrounded by other Victorian homes that exuded "old money."

As I trotted up the steps, a lovely older couple who I assumed were the owners greeted me. They appeared to be in their early sixties. The man had salt-and-pepper hair and a mustache. He was only slightly taller than his wife and was wearing tan slacks and a long-sleeve, plaid shirt. The woman had gray hair and glasses. She was slightly plump around the middle and was wearing a long-sleeve, button-up blouse and a long, flowy skirt. Their infectious smiles invited me in long before I reached the top step.

"Callie St. Claire, I presume?" the woman asked.

"That's me, ma'am."

"Oh, call me Marie. This is my husband, Carl." Marie motioned to the man standing next to her.

"Nice to meet you, Callie." He held out his hand.

"Nice to meet you, too, sir." I shook his outstretched hand.

"Please, call me Carl. Let me help you with your bags." He took hold of the bags I had set on the porch next to me.

"Thank you," I said. The couple ushered me inside. My eyes darted around in every direction of the foyer, and I spun around, awestruck. "This is one of the most beautiful homes I have ever seen."

The home was decorated with red and white floral wallpaper that would cause most people to vomit in their mouths, but I loved it. There wasn't a vast amount of furniture due to the narrow width and long length before entering the dining room, which was located just behind the beginning of the grand staircase with the cherry wood stairs and banister. The air hinted of chocolate chip cookies that may have been baked earlier that day.

"You must be hungry and tired after such a long drive. Would you like something to eat? I know it's late, but we have some leftovers from supper if you'd like." Marie draped her arm over my shoulders.

I normally would have been uncomfortable and shied away from the contact, but with Marie, for some reason, I felt at ease. I didn't understand it, but I welcomed it all the same. "If it's not too much trouble." My cheeks warmed from her kindness.

"No trouble at all. Carl will show you to your room, and by the time you get settled, I'll have some supper for you."

"Follow me." Carl motioned as he started up the stairs with my bags.

"Are you sure I can't help you with those?" I asked.

As we ascended the stairs, my hand glided up the railing to the second floor. The banister had a smooth, glossy finish that smelled like Old English furniture polish. I breathed deep as the scent transported me back to my childhood home just after my mom had polished the furniture. The memory brought a smile to my lips and a tear to my eye.

"And here we are," Carl informed me as he opened the door to the room just off the staircase.

I stepped into the room, and my breath lodged in my throat. It was as if I had traveled back in time to the 1800s. To my left sat a cherry wood king-size canopy bed. It was covered with a blue and white checkered patch quilt. The canopy was made of white lace with diamond shapes hanging down. A light blue velvet chaise lounge sat along the wall to the right, and nestled in the bay window overlooking the neighborhood was a small writing desk made of the same wood as the bed. The same vomit-inducing wallpaper as in the foyer, except in light blue, covered the walls. Some Impressionist paintings that adorned the walls reminded me of Monet landscapes. The dresser and night table were the same dark wood as the bed and desk. The small lamp resting on the night table wore a white Victorian-style shade and appeared to be an old oil lantern repurposed into an electrical lamp. I had images of a room filled with a warm glow from the lamp dancing in my head.

"Is it to your liking?

"Are you kidding me? It's perfect!" I giggled like a little girl being shown her newly decorated room. My mom used to tell me I was born in the wrong era because I loved everything antique or of the Victorian variety.

"Glad you like it." Carl chuckled. "Make yourself at home and come down to the kitchen when you're ready."

"Thank you so much, Carl."

After the door was closed securely, I sighed dreamily, plopped one of the bags on the bed, and unzipped it. I hung my clothes in the closet and tucked the rest into the dresser before my belly bellowed, long and loud. I placed my hand on my stomach and headed downstairs. I strolled into the kitchen and found myself alone.

"That didn't take long," Marie spoke up from behind me.

I jumped and spun around, my eyes wide. Holy moly!

Marie placed her hand over her mouth. "Sorry. I have a bad habit of sneaking up on people without realizing I'm sneaking up on them."

If she only knew how many times my aunt would lie in hiding, waiting to pounce. Sometimes laughing. Sometimes growing angry if I showed fear. Sometimes livid if I didn't. I couldn't win—Aunt Carla made sure of it.

I slowed my racing heart, planted a fake smile on my face, and shrugged. "I don't have that much stuff." Heat engorged my cheeks. Darn it. No matter how hard I tried to hide my feelings, they always showed up on my face. Traitors.

"Well, have a seat, and I'll get your plate." Marie pulled out a chair for me at the big dining room table.

I had never seen a dining room table quite that large before. It brought to mind images of a table one would find in a royal palace—at least in the movies I had seen anyway. It was dark wood, just like the other furniture I had seen in the inn. It was sturdy, secure, and beautiful. I couldn't help but wonder if there was a correlation between the type of wood and the owners of the inn. Would they become permanent fixtures—sturdy and secure—in my time in Edenton?

Back to the table, though. I ran my hands along the routered, rounded edges of the table. What would it be like full of people? What types of people had sat around this table? Oh, the stories Marie and Carl must have. A few minutes later, Marie appeared from the kitchen with a plate full of mashed potatoes and meatloaf. The aromas of melted butter and garlic wafted on the air, and my stomach rumbled loud enough to wake the dead.

"Oh my! You'd better eat up." Marie chuckled as she set the plate in front of me. "I didn't know if you like gravy, so I put it on the side for you."

"Thank you so much. This looks amazing. It's been a long time since I've had a home-cooked meal. I really appreciate it."

Marie cocked her head before nodding and exiting the

7

room.

It was true. I hadn't enjoyed a home-cooked meal since before I went to live with my aunt. Cooking was not my forte, and my aunt only fixed meals of the frozen variety. When I was on my own, I continued consuming frozen dinners or takeout. Cooking for one only reinforced my pathetic circumstances. I was alone, and I always would be. I unfolded the napkin, placed it over my lap, and bowed my head to give thanks to God for the food. I took my first bite, and the meatloaf practically disintegrated on my tongue. My mom's cooking instantly came to mind. Oh, how I wish I could have gone back and spent more time with her and let her teach me to cook. I breathed deeply, willing back the tears that formed any time I thought of my mom or dad.

I had grown accustomed to eating alone as I had done so since my parents died. My aunt made me eat in my room every night as if I wasn't worthy of sitting at her table. She had told me as much. At school, for quite a while, I sat in exile during the lunch period. My friends slowly distanced themselves from my life. No idea why. After so long, I just gave up on people and stopped trying. Before I knew it, I had finished everything on my plate. I sighed, picked up my dishes, and took them to the kitchen. Neither Marie nor Carl was anywhere to be found, so I searched out a dishrag and some dish soap.

"Don't you dare!" a voice boomed from behind me, making my heart stop. I turned to see Marie standing in the doorway with her hands on her hips. Her stance reminded me of my mom when she was about to scoff at me. "Guests do not do the dishes."

"I'm . . . I'm sorry," I stammered. I still had trouble when people corrected me. I always waited for the hit to come. I must have flinched because Marie rushed to my side and wrapped her arm around my shoulders.

"Oh, sweetie. It's okay. I didn't mean to upset you."

"I'm sorry. I spent the last years of my childhood doing the dishes . . . all the cleaning, really. It's just become second nature," I confessed.

"I can certainly understand that. How about you wash, and I'll dry and put them away?"

She couldn't possibly understand, but I just kept quiet about that. No one needed to know *that* secret. Not until I felt someone could be trusted with it, anyway. "Okay."

There weren't that many dishes, so with the two of us, it seemed to take mere seconds to do. As I rinsed out the dish cloth, I let out a yawn I didn't realize I was holding in.

"Why don't you let me finish up here, and you go get some rest, dear?"

"Okay. Thank you again, Marie," I told her before turning to trudge up the stairs and stifling another yawn. I just didn't have the energy to argue. After the long drive and all the emotions surging through me, sleep sounded amazing.

Once I got into my room and closed the door, I flopped on the bed from sheer exhaustion. I guess that eleven-and-a-half-hour drive wore me out more than I thought as dreamland overtook me.

Chapter 2

Callie

The next morning, I woke with a start. My pulse raced—the dream of my parents fresh in my mind. In the dream, I continually see them fading away, calling and reaching out to me. I hadn't had that dream in a long time, so I didn't know why it had started again. It was frustrating. I thought the change of scenery would change how I slept. I guess I was wrong. That, or maybe it just took time. Maybe it was the fact that the fourteenth anniversary of their deaths was fast approaching. The terrible day always arrived before I was ready.

I ran my hands over my face, glanced at the small alarm clock on the nightstand, and slid out from under the covers. I peeked out the window and surveyed the neighborhood in the morning light. It was just as beautiful when cascaded by the sunshine. A couple walked their small, black dog, and a child rode his bike down the sidewalk. I shuffled into the bathroom inside my suite to hop in the shower. I needed to go to the library to use their computers to search for a job.

After I felt presentable, I made my way down the stairs knowing I had already missed breakfast as it was almost ten o'clock. I was hoping, though, there was something I could grab.

"Good morning, Callie," Carl greeted me from the bottom

of the stairs.

"Morning." I grinned down at him.

"Breakfast is over, but there are some muffins in the kitchen if you're hungry. Feel free to help yourself."

"Thank you." I started for the kitchen before turning back around. "Carl, could you tell me how to get to the library?"

"Sure. Turn left right here at the corner. That's Broad Street. Go down Broad Street until you get to the street just after Courageous Café and Bakery. That's Water Street. You want to turn right, and the library will be on the right. It's about a ten- to fifteen-minute walk from here, so it's not far."

"Thank you so much." I turned and continued to the kitchen.

I snatched a muffin that smelled sinfully delicious. I glanced back at the smorgasbord of muffins splayed before me. I stretched out my hand to grab another muffin or two but snatched my hand back as if I had been scalded by hot water. *No, Callie. You don't have to stuff your face to make you happy. You are starting a new life. It starts with what and how much you put in your mouth.*

"Thanks for the muffin, Marie. I'll see you later," I told her and bounded out the door.

I slipped the other strap of my backpack onto my shoulder and decided it was too beautiful of a day to drive, so I strolled down Broad Street on foot. Plus, it would give me a little bit of exercise. I needed to be more active in this new life. I noticed all the cute shops and local eateries. I wanted to experience them all.

Courageous Café and Bakery beckoned me to go inside. I stuffed some more of the muffin in my mouth and threw the rest in the garbage can. It was too delicious to waste *all* of it. I opened the door to the jingling bells announcing my arrival. Some of the patrons glanced in my direction but quickly returned to their conversations. I always felt self-conscious being a big girl going into an eatery such as a bakery. I felt like people were judging me. I didn't get that feeling in this one, though. The air was filled with the scents of pastries and coffee. I inhaled deeply.

"Welcome to Courageous Café and Bakery," a cute, young, petite girl of about sixteen or seventeen said from the opposite side of the counter. "How can I help you?"

Her pretty smile warmed me like sunshine. With her long, wispy, blonde hair, with ringlets at the ends, cascading down her back and with her sparkling blue eyes, she reminded me of a Precious Moments figurine. I read her nametag before glancing up. "Hi, Caitlyn. I'll take a hot chocolate, please." I drank hot chocolate like most people drank coffee. I hated coffee. Yuck!

It wasn't long before Caitlyn arrived back at the counter with my hot chocolate in hand.

"You aren't hiring by chance, are you?" I asked, wringing my hands. I figured it wouldn't hurt to ask while I was there and before I lost the courage to ask.

"I'm not sure. Let me go get my mom."

"Thank you."

A few seconds later, a woman resembling Caitlyn sauntered to the counter. "Hi," she greeted with an outstretched hand. "I'm Marci."

I grasped her hand and shook. Not too hard, not too soft, and not too long—just like my dad taught me. "Hi, Marci. I just moved here and was wondering if you are hiring at all."

"Unfortunately, not right now." Even though I tried my hardest to hide my disappointment, my shoulders slumped. "Why don't you leave your name and number with me, and I'll call you if anything changes."

I scribbled my name and number on the piece of paper Marci had given me. Of course, it couldn't be *that* easy. Nothing ever was for me, so I wasn't sure why I thought it would be any different with a change in geography. I grabbed a seat by the window at the front of the café to drink my hot chocolate. The window also let me enjoy people-watching.

I scanned the café and bakery. It had bright colors everywhere. It was a place that a person could go to and be instantly uplifted by the cheery décor. It wasn't long before my eyes landed on lettering painted on the wall. *BE STRONG AND COURAGEOUS.* I knew that particular scripture well. It had become somewhat of a mantra of mine when I was living with my aunt. I had to be strong and courageous to deal with the beatings that took place on an almost daily basis.

I continued to sip my hot chocolate as people came and went. The drink slid down my throat, hot and silky. I observed Caitlyn and Marci chatting with customers. I could tell they loved working there. They seemed to know everyone with whom they came in contact. I overheard them ask about children and family members. I could see the delight in everyone's faces as they talked and laughed with one another.

After leaving the café, I decided to spend some time exploring the town. I continued down Broad Street to Edenton Bay, the body of water on which Edenton was nestled. The aroma of fish mixed with the briny scent of salt and mossy vegetation coming off the water reminded me of the lakes back in Indiana. Most of the townspeople were wearing shorts and T-shirts. I was wearing jeans and a T-shirt. I had never been comfortable wearing shorts because my legs were so chunky, short, and glaring white.

I made my way onto the pier that stretched out in front of the white lighthouse with a red roof and black shutters. It was so beautiful there. I could see myself spending time at the water's edge. Oh, how the lighthouse must have been a beacon for those out at sea, guiding them to the safety and security of dry land. Isn't that what God had done for me? He had shown His light and guided me to this place, much like that lighthouse. My eyes began to mist, and I delighted in the thought. I had that reaction whenever I thought about God and His grace and mercy. I had been in Edenton for less than a day, and already I was happier than I had been in quite some time. For the first time in fourteen years, I felt so free. I closed my eyes and let the breeze caress my face. It felt wonderful.

When I heard a boat approaching, I opened my eyes to see it was a tour boat. I hadn't been on a boat since my childhood, and I always had a good time out on the water. I walked to the end of the pier, past departing passengers, and paid to join the next tour. I wasn't excited to be in close quarters with people I didn't know, but I wanted to go out onto the water, so I just had to suck it up.

The boat was red and cream colored with a canopy on top to shelter us from the glaring sun. The ride out into the bay was relaxing. The water was calm, and the breeze across my face was welcomed. Most of the passengers sat toward the back, so I sat near the front. I wanted to soak in as much information as I possibly could. I wanted to learn everything I could about the town of Edenton.

The captain of the vessel captivated us with fascinating stories about Edenton and the bay. "You probably never heard of the old cypress tree here in the bay. Legend has it that when a ship came into Edenton, it was customary for the master to put a bottle of the best rum in the hollow trunk. Then, when a ship left the bay, they would stop at the old tree and drink to a safe voyage." The tour lasted about forty-five minutes.

As I got off the boat once it was docked, I saw the library off to the northwest. "I guess I'd better get some job searching done," I mumbled as I headed in that direction. I had to walk past Town Hall to get to the library that was directly behind it but across the street.

The library was a brick building with white pillars running up to a white triangle canopy with a couple of steps leading up to the green front door. Large picture windows took up either side of the entrance. It was bigger on the inside than I had imagined. It was colorful, with rows and rows of stacks, every shelf filled with books. I loved the musty smell of old books. I would never get pure joy reading from an electronic device like I did when I was holding a book in my hands.

I asked the young girl at the front desk if I could use the computers. She looked at me as if I sprouted an extra head. "Just sign your name here, and the computers are over there." She motioned toward the corner.

The computer area was a ghost town. I wasn't surprised as I figured everyone used their own laptops, tablets, or phones. I only had a little flip phone so my job could reach me. Well, when I had a job, that is. I didn't see the need for anything more because I didn't have any family or friends. The friends that hadn't distanced themselves after my parents died were run off by my aunt. My aunt was the only family I had left, and I wanted to be as far away from her as possible. As I became an adult, I had lost confidence in people and just didn't want to get hurt anymore, so I had steered clear. I sat down at a computer, and my eyes were drawn to the corkboard on the wall. A flyer for a grief group caught my attention. I bit my bottom lip as I read it.

Lord, help me. I don't know if I should risk going to this kind of meeting. I sat in silence for a few minutes.

You can't step out into the fullness of the Light with one foot stuck in the darkness. You have to let go of past hurts and truly forgive those who caused them. Not just a sound bite but the forgiveness that comes from deep within. From Me. And you have to learn to forgive yourself also. You are My daughter, and I love you.

I was startled by the revelation, but I knew it was God. I knew instantly what I had to do, like it or not. I sighed deeply, then stood to take a closer look. The flyer said the group was meeting that evening at six in the library conference room. I returned to my seat and took my notebook and pen out of my bag. I made a note about the meeting before proceeding to search for available jobs in the area.

After a few hours of exploring, with no luck, I gave up. I glanced at the clock on the computer, and my stomach grumbled—time for lunch. I packed up my things and headed back up Broad Street. I passed some small shops selling a variety of items from clothing to Christian gifts. Benches adorned almost every corner.

I came to a stop at C'est La Vie Bistro. It had a striped awning and black-framed windows. A few cast-iron tables and chairs sat outside for patrons who wanted to enjoy the outdoors while eating. Everything about the town resembled every small-town Hallmark movie I had ever watched. I loved every bit of it. I couldn't get over the feeling I was finally home. I opened the door, inhaled, and was immediately bombarded with the aroma of chicken, garlic, and oregano. My mouth watered.

"Have a seat wherever you'd like, and I'll be right with ya," a friendly, bubbly waitress said before skirting away to deliver food to a table full of hungry-looking men.

I snagged the first empty table I could find. The place was

packed for lunch. As I slid into the booth, my eyes were drawn to the table of men, where I found two steely-blue eyes staring back at me. When my eyes met his, neither of us looked away. The man flashed a half-grin that made my heart skip a beat before returning his attention to his food and the others at his table. I picked up a menu to both hide the redness that I was sure had taken up residence on my face and to decide what I wanted to order.

"Hi there. My name is Olivia, and I'll be taking care of ya today," my waitress told me with a slight southern drawl.

One of everything on the menu is what I wanted to tell her but definitely wasn't going to when those blue eyes kept gazing in my direction. No way! Food had always been my constant companion. Luckily, I hadn't gained *too* much weight after my parents died. Maybe because my aunt rationed my food? I would slay this demon, or I'd die trying.

I gave Olivia a once-over. She had chin-length, straight, light-brown hair, brown eyes, a thin body, and an olive complexion. She was the type of woman I had always envied. She was what most men would have considered the picture of perfection.

"Hi, Olivia. What's good here?"

"Everything, of course. The spaghetti is my favorite, though."

"Mmm. I love spaghetti. I'll have that." I flashed a quick grin as I handed her the menu.

"And to drink?"

"I'll just have a water, please."

"Comin' right up."

"Thank you."

I couldn't help but glance back over at the table of men. Once again, I found those blue-gray eyes staring back at me. I quickly diverted my gaze. I didn't know why he kept looking at me. I didn't know if he thought something bad about me or what. I wasn't sure what to do with myself while I waited for my food, so I gazed out the window at the people passing by and took in the atmosphere of the restaurant. The tables were made of black wood. The walls were a mustard yellow with bright, multicolored paintings. It wasn't long before Olivia returned with my order.

As soon as she set the plate in front of me, Olivia asked, "You're new here, aren't ya?"

"Yeah, is it that obvious?" Heat rushed to my cheeks.

"No. It's just a small town, and I've lived here my whole life, and I know I don't know ya." She chuckled.

"Well, that makes sense." I laughed. "I just got here last night." I stared down at my entangled hands resting on my lap.

"Are ya looking for work?"

"Yes, as a matter of fact, I am. Do you know of anything? I haven't had much luck so far." Heat danced around my cheeks once more.

"Yeah. We're lookin' for another server. Ya interested?"

"Absolutely. Thank you." Excitement bubbled up inside me, but I managed to maintain my composure. I really wanted to shout with glee.

"I'll bring ya an application. Enjoy your lunch," she told me as she hurried to wait on other patrons.

I placed my napkin in my lap and bowed my head to pray. I hadn't always been a Christian. In fact, I stayed mad at God for a long time for taking my parents away from me. It took time to realize that God's timing wasn't my timing. When I went to live with my aunt, who I had dubbed "Cruella," I needed something to give me hope and solid ground. I didn't have any friends, but one day at lunch, a girl in my grade,

18

Jennie, told me about the relationship I could have with God. I had never known I could have that. We ended up sitting together at lunch every day after that. Eventually, I accepted Jesus into my life. My life wasn't the same after. I put my hope in the Lord to get me through my hardest time. I prayed constantly for Him to show me what He wanted for my life. I lived for that moment—when I would know exactly what He had for me. I hoped it was here in Edenton.

As I ate my lunch, the smell of the garlic and oregano from the spaghetti invaded my nose. It tasted heavenly. My mind drifted to daydreams of what my life might look like in this town. Making my daydreams a reality would be hard, but I hoped I could make it happen. I dreamed of buying a small house with a fenced yard surrounding it. Maybe I would get a pet as well. I had always wanted one but never had one aside from my aunt's cats.

"Ma'am, are ya all finished?" Olivia's voice had me jumping back to the present. "Oh, I'm so sorry. I didn't mean ta scare ya."

When Olivia rested her hand on my shoulder, I shied away. I wasn't much for physical contact. My aunt had given me enough physical contact to last a lifetime. "It's okay. I just got lost in thought. Yes. I'm done."

"I brought ya an application."

"Thank you so much. Is it okay if I fill it out here?"

"For sure."

Olivia skirted away, and I dug in my backpack for my pen. I filled out the application and left it on the table with my payment for my food. I still had a few hours before the grief group, so I decided to check out the shops along Broad Street. Some of the shops, I just glanced in the window, while others, I explored inside. I found so many things I would have loved to buy, but without a home to call my own, I didn't make any purchases. Yet.

After perusing the shops, I settled on going to the library to wait for the meeting time. Nothing really made me happier than getting lost in a good book. The library came into view, and my stomach did a flip-flop. My nerves about the meeting had my hands sweating and my heart rate increasing. I had never really talked about my parents' deaths. Mainly, it was because whenever I tried to talk about my feelings surrounding their deaths, I was told it was time to get over it or to stop feeling sorry for myself. I had to go to the meeting. It was the beginning of a new life, and I had to completely let go of the grief and sadness that plagued me for far too long. I had to do it to step into my future by having both feet in the present, not the past.

I stood at the entrance of the library, willing myself to go inside. My feet felt as if they were covered in cement. I inhaled, wiped my hands on my pants, exhaled, and opened the door. I navigated my way by following the signs to the Christian Romance section to find a book before sitting down in an oversized, fluffy chair. I got lost in the world Karen Kingsbury created in one of her Baxter family books.

At 5:55 p.m., I stood from the comfort of the chair, laid my book in the return bin, and ambled to the conference room. I had seen the sign earlier for the group meeting. I grabbed the door handle and let out the breath I was holding in. "Here goes nothing," I mumbled and pulled open the door.

I crept in with all the confidence I could muster, which wasn't much, and sunk into the first empty chair I found. The chairs were arranged in a circle, so it made it impossible for me to be invisible, which was exactly what I wanted. I hated being the center of attention. It made my anxiety skyrocket. There was nowhere to hide. My hands began to sweat, and my heart started to pound. I was certain it was loud enough for those around me to hear, but luckily, everyone was too engrossed in conversations to notice. I closed my eyes and exhaled, trying my best to calm my nerves.

Chapter 3

Colton Andrews

I noticed her the minute she opened the door. I had seen her earlier at the Bistro. Those emerald-green eyes and that fiery, unruly hair captivated me. Her hair reminded me of Julia Roberts in *Pretty Woman*. Who was this beautiful woman with such sad eyes? I grew up here and knew everyone, and she was a mystery—a mystery I wanted to solve.

"Colt, are ya with me?" Jon, my best friend, nudged me with his shoulder.

"Oh, yeah, sorry." I snapped out of the spell she had me under.

"Looks like we gotta new person. Why don't ya give her a name tag and introduce yerself?" Jon shoved a name tag and Sharpie in my hand.

I strutted over to where she was sitting. My palms started to sweat, so I wiped them on my pants. I sat in the next seat. *Calm yourself, Colt.*

"Hi. I'm Colt." I extended my hand. What I knew had to be a goofy grin spread across my face.

She first looked at my hand, and then her eyes made their way up to mine. I thought I saw recognition flash through hers. She grinned, but it didn't reach all the way to her eyes. I tried to gain a deeper view into the green sea, but she darted her gaze to the floor. Sadness crept over me. I wasn't sure why, but it did all the same. Was she uncomfortable with me? With being in groups? Maybe it was with herself? Perhaps it was all three? Even though I didn't know this woman, I wanted to find out. I wanted to help her.

"Here's a name tag for ya. Write only your first name."

"Okay. Thank you." She took the name tag and marker from my hand, her gaze not moving off the carpet. Her leg jiggled.

"Ya move here or just passing through?" I ran my fingers through my hair and rubbed the back of my neck. It was what I did every time I was nervous or uncomfortable. But why was I so nervous around her? I didn't even know her name.

She rubbed one foot over the other. "You're the second person to ask me something like that today."

I chuckled. She had some skills when it came to avoiding answering my questions. "Small town. Everyone knows everyone."

She nodded, still not looking at me. Her leg pumped faster. "I see that."

I was clearly making her uncomfortable. Not my intention. Especially not here. "Well, welcome to the group . . . and Edenton." I did my best not to display the same goofy grin on my face.

She glanced my way and formed her lips into what had to be the most forced smile I had ever seen. "Thank you."

I sauntered back over to where Jon was standing and berated myself silently. *Way to go, Colt. She probably thinks you're a stalker or something.*

Jon and I had been best friends our entire lives. When I lost my dad, and then he lost the love of his life, we founded this group. Even though we encouraged people to share their experiences, I never had. I just hadn't ever felt ready to bare my soul like that, even though everyone knew how my dad died. Small town. They didn't know the whole story, though.

"Okay, everyone," Jon's voice boomed through the room. "Let's find our seats and get started."

I sat across from her. She glanced in my direction, and my stomach did a somersault. It had been a long time since a woman had that effect on me. Jon took the seat next to me and began the meeting.

"Since we have some new faces this week, let's go around and introduce ourselves."

Everyone's eyes turned to her. A blush formed on her face as she squirmed in her seat. She didn't like being the center of attention—I made a mental note.

"I'll go ahead and start. My name is Jon."

"Welcome, Jon," everyone said in unison.

It wasn't long before I felt Jon's elbow in my side, which produced a round of chuckles from the group.

"Oh, I'm Colt."

"Welcome, Colt."

She twisted her hands as each person spoke their name, her turn getting closer. I couldn't wait to hear her sweet voice again.

"Um. Hi. I'm. Um. Callie," she stammered with a strained smile.

"Welcome, Callie."

Her body relaxed and slumped down in her chair after the attention moved past her. Her gaze made its way over to me once again. I tried to tear my eyes away but was transfixed to hers. She gave me a hint of a grin before her eyes left mine.

"Okay. Thank y'all. This is a place of support and under-standing, no judgments. We have all been through some sort of loss. Callie, since you are new, would ya like to share with the group why you're here?"

Callie looked at Jon with wide eyes.

"Ya don't have to," Jon quickly added with his hands out.

"No," she said quietly, sitting a little straighter in her chair. She stared at her hands. "I need to. It's part of why I'm here."

I placed my elbows on my knees so I could hold on to her words.

"My parents died at the same time fourteen years ago . . ."

Gasps could be heard around the room. I couldn't even begin to imagine losing both my parents *and* on the same day.

"It was my sixteenth birthday. My parents were coming home from their trip to England so they could surprise me. Their flight left Newark, New Jersey to stop in Chicago where my parents were going to drive from Chicago to our home in Indianapolis." She inhaled deeply as a tear made a path down her cheek. She wiped it away before it dripped from her chin. "I'm sorry. I've never really talked about this before."

"Take your time," Jon reassured her with a calm, caring tone.

"Well, you see, it's all my fault they died. If it hadn't been my birthday, they wouldn't have been on that plane . . ." Callie exhaled, and her shoulders shook as she sobbed before running out the door.

Before Jon could tell me it was okay to go, I shot out of my chair and bolted out of the room. I had no idea if I would find her. Racing out to the parking lot, I found her crying on the curb. I sat down next to her. I slowly wrapped my arm around her shoulder. I expected her to shy away or flinch, but she didn't.

"Callie," I whispered. "It's not your fault."

She latched on and cried harder. I held her close until her tears subsided. I didn't know much about consoling women, but having her in my arms felt like the most natural thing I had ever done. I had no idea how long we had been sitting out there, but since no one had come out from the meeting, I guessed it hadn't been long.

"I'm so so so sorry." She moved away and wiped her face dry with the backs of her hands. "You must think I'm a hot mess. You'd think after fourteen years, I wouldn't have this strong of a reaction just talking about them."

"Not at all. We all heal in different ways and different amounts of time." This is one of the reasons I never talked about the death of my dad. I knew I would be a . . . what was the term she just used? Hot mess?

My arms suddenly felt empty without her in them. I didn't understand my reaction to this woman I didn't even know, but I liked it.

"Can I give ya a ride home?" I second-guessed my question as soon as it left my mouth. *What are you thinking? Why would she take a ride home with someone she doesn't even know? Way to be a real creeper, Colt.* As far as being a hot mess goes, I didn't think that at all. I thought she was one of the most beautiful women I had ever seen. Whoa! Where did that come from?

"Normally, I would say no, but I walked here, and I think I'm too drained to walk back. I'm staying at Edenton Inn."

"Okay. Let's get ya back then."

I stood, grabbed her hands, and pulled her up off the curb. Electricity surged through my body. It was almost more than I could handle, but when her hands fell from mine, the electric charge left as quickly as it had arrived.

"Um. My truck is over here." I suddenly didn't know exactly what to say.

I opened the passenger side door and assisted Callie up

before closing it and darting around the truck to climb in the other side.

"So, when did ya move here?"

"Yesterday," she whispered.

"Do ya know where you're going to live?"

"Just the inn for now." She fidgeted with her hands.

"I know we don't know each other, but I have plenty of room at my ranch."

What are you doing, Colt? You don't invite women to the ranch, especially one you don't know. This woman had me saying things I never say. I couldn't understand it at all. I just kept feeling like I was sounding more and more like a psycho.

"Thank you, but I'm okay at the inn for now."

"Well, at least come by and take a look before ya say no." I grinned at her. *Why are you practically begging this woman to live at the ranch?* I shook the question from my head.

"Okay. I'll think about it."

"What's your number? I'll text ya the address."

"Why don't you just give me the address? I can write it down."

There she goes skillfully dodging my questions again. "Okay. Well, then here's my card. Address and phone number are there. Call me or stop by anytime ya like."

Callie took the card from my hand. When we drove up to the inn, I wasn't ready for our conversation to end or for her to get out of the truck. "Thank you for . . . well, everything," she said.

She peeked at me for the first time since leaving the library. My pulse quickened as my eyes met hers. The only things I saw reflected in her eyes were sadness and loneliness. I knew both sentiments very well. I wanted to replace those with other things, like love and happiness. What? I wanted to know what her eyes showed when her smile actually reached them.

Callie slid out of the truck, strolled up to the door, and disappeared inside. To my dismay, she never turned back around. I wanted her to so badly. Isn't that what women do? They get to the door, turn around, and wave before going inside? Maybe they only do that when they are interested. My shoulders slumped at the thought. I was completely losing it. I shook my head and chuckled before driving back to the library.

Chapter 4

Callie

The inn was quiet when I stepped inside. I was relieved. As much as I liked Marie and Carl, I just wasn't up for conversation. I felt the same as I did when I learned my parents were dead—exhausted and empty. I hurried to my room and only exhaled once the door was closed securely behind me. I needed to process everything from the meeting, especially the guy.

Colt was his name? He was the guy I had a staring contest with at the Bistro at lunch. Those blue eyes with his jet-black hair drew me in like no other. Swoon-worthy, really. They literally took my breath away. It's why I had trouble getting words out when he was around. I hadn't realized just how tall he was until he plucked me up off the curb, and I was standing in front of him. He was almost a foot taller than my five-foot-five-inch height. Heat rushed to my cheeks as I thought about how I had clung to him and allowed some of the grief to finally escape. I placed my hands over my face. I wanted to lie about my name. I thought sharing my name was too personal, but I just couldn't do it. My mouth opened to say another name, but mine flew out. It was for the best, though. Last year, on my twenty-ninth birthday, I made a promise to God that I would re-dedicate my life to living with Him at the center. I had strayed for many years because I felt I had to do certain things to not be alone. I just lost sight of what truly mattered in life—God. So, lying wasn't something I could bring myself to do, no matter the cost.

"Colt must think I'm a complete moron," I mumbled and rolled my eyes. Why didn't I just give him my number? I knew why. He would see my ancient flip phone and make fun of me like everyone else always had. Maybe being in this town would make me consider an upgrade. As I got ready for bed, I remembered the current of electricity that surged its way up my arms as he helped me off the curb. Did he feel it, too? I was too afraid to look into his eyes. I didn't want to see the pity I was sure resided there. I wasn't sure how to feel about the tumble my stomach took each time our eyes met. I had never had a response to a man quite like that before. I lay in bed, twirling the business card between my fingers.

I knew in my heart I would go see Colt the next day, but my head told me I should steer clear. It was actually my aunt in my head telling me to stay far away. She would always tell me men were nothing but trouble and that they would only cause me pain. She would then follow up with how I wouldn't have to worry about that because no man would ever want a woman like me, no matter how pretty my face was. Maybe this one time, I could allow my heart and feelings to take the lead. But what if what I thought was between us was my overactive imagination and wishful thinking? What if my aunt was right? What if no man would ever love me because I was stuck in my fat body? I soon drifted off to sleep with those thoughts swirling around in my head.

Chapter 5

Colt

After I dropped Callie off at the inn, I made my way back to the library. I couldn't get her out of my head or the scent of her out of my nose. She intrigued me. I wanted to know more. I wanted to know everything, really.

"Where'd ya go?" Jon asked as soon as I stepped through the door.

"Sorry, man. I gave Callie a ride home. Sorry to leave in the middle . . ." I trailed off.

"Say no more. I saw the way ya looked at her at the Bistro and here."

I sighed. "I invited her to the ranch." I ran my fingers through my hair and wrapped my hand around the back of my neck.

"What? Ya don't invite women out there. Thought ya said it's your safe space."

"I know." I sighed again. "The words were out of my mouth before I knew what I was saying."

"Do ya think she'll come?" Jon knew me well enough to know the invitation wasn't just for a visit.

"I don't know. For the most part, I really hope so."

"And the other part?"

I glanced over at Jon, and he held up his hands in surrender.

"Let's get this room put back together so we can get out of here," I suggested.

Jon and I were such good friends that I asked him to help me run Redemption Ranch. My dad had passed away a few years before, and my mom couldn't bring herself to stay, so she moved to Florida after signing the ranch over to me. Oh, how I missed them both. I turned it into more than just a ranch, though. It was a place of second chances. It was a place where horses and people alike could find redemption from whatever life had thrown their way. We built cabins on the property for those who needed a home, and in exchange, they worked on the ranch. I loved every minute of it. I felt it was what God had called me to do. God extended His mercy, forgiveness, and grace to me, so it was my turn to pay it forward and extend the same things to others who needed it and tell them about a God who loves them no matter where they are in life.

It took me a long time to get to a place of acceptance on so many things—my dad's death, my mom's leaving, the feelings of being abandoned, and being single. Just to name a few. Whatever God had for my life was what I wanted, too. No matter the cost.

After I dropped Jon off at his cabin, I drove down the dirt road to my house. That night, for some reason, it felt so empty. I hadn't felt that alone since my mom left, but that night, I did. I hadn't brought myself to move into the master bedroom. I didn't know why for sure. Maybe it was because I would always see it as my parents' room, but if God ever saw to it to bring a woman into my life, I would. The dawn brought a new day with a lot to accomplish, so I climbed into bed and succumbed to sleep.

Chapter 6

Callie

I was up and ready to go bright and early as the rays of sunshine streamed through the sheer undrawn curtains, bathing me in the morning light. I checked my phone for messages because I realized I didn't even look at it the day before. I had missed a call. In the message, the man's voice said that if I wanted to come to the Bistro for an interview, to call him back. Shoot! I hoped I didn't miss my chance. I really needed a job. I would stop by while I was out. I still had most of the trust my parents left me, but I didn't want to use it if I could work to pay for my expenses.

I put my wet hair in a tight bun. I stepped into my black slacks and navy-blue blouse. I applied some foundation and mascara before leaving my room. I was never one to wear a lot of makeup. It always felt caked on, and I didn't like that feeling. I hoped my choices were good enough to get the job or, at the very least, an interview.

"Morning, Marie." I waved as I strode into the kitchen. My heart seemed to feel a little lighter. Different. Happier. Was this what the beginning of healing felt like? I sure hoped so.

The aroma of banana muffins struck my nose. They lined the counter, and I couldn't resist snatching one, warmth emitting through the paper liner. Muffins and pastries had always been my weakness. I broke a piece off and popped it in my mouth.

"Mmm. If heaven had a taste, I think this would be it." I closed my eyes and savored the taste on my tongue.

Marie grinned. "Have you heard from the Bistro yet?"

"Yeah. They called yesterday, but I missed it. I'm gonna stop by there before I head out to Redemption Ranch."

Marie's smile grew.

"What?" I tossed another piece of muffin in my mouth.

"Nothing. You just must have met Colt Andrews."

"Maybe." I felt my cheeks grow warm. "I should get going."

"Have a great day!" Marie called after me in a sing-song voice.

What was that about? Colt Andrews must have quite the reputation around here. Shrugging it off, I drove to the Bistro, hoping to get an interview but didn't know if I could since I didn't return the man's phone call. After parking in a space right out front, I inhaled, jumped down, pasted on my best grin, and sauntered through the door.

"Callie?" A woman's voice called out.

"Yes?" I turned around, wondering who knew my name. "Oh, hi, Olivia. How are you?" She must have looked at my application for my name.

"Livin' the dream. How are you?"

"I'm great. Thanks. I got a call yesterday about an interview? I meant to call back, but it was a busy day, and I didn't get the message until it was too late, so I thought I'd just stop by."

"Oh, let me go get Jesse. He's the owner."

"Okay." I turned and peered out the window.

"Callie?" A baritone voice with a deep southern drawl boomed from behind me. Warmth spread from the richness of his tone.

"Hi," I responded as I turned around.

"Nice to meet ya. I'm Jesse." He extended his hand.

"Nice to meet you also." I took his hand and shook it just like my dad had taught me.

The memory of my dad made my mouth form what I was sure was a goofy grin. He had taught me a lot of things about job interviews. He is the reason I'd gotten every job I'd ever had. A slight sizzle at the point of contact with Jesse fizzled out before it could even move to my wrist. It was nothing compared to the electricity I had felt when Colt had touched me.

"Why don't we have a seat?" Jesse motioned to a table.

"Sure."

Jesse asked question after question. He was a handsome guy with light blond hair, chocolate brown eyes, and a square jaw. He had a defined upper body . . . *Focus, Callie. Geez!*

"When can ya start?"

I glanced up at him and saw what I never imagined I would see directed at me. It was the expression a man gave a woman when he thought she was desirable. *Get that notion out of your head. There is no way he thinks that way about you.* My aunt's voice was in my head again. Always in my head.

"Um . . . Now?"

"Great! Do ya have jeans? I'll go get ya a uniform shirt. What size?"

"Yes, and extra-large, please." The all-to-familiar heat crept to my cheeks.

Jesse stood from the table and disappeared into the back of the restaurant. I couldn't believe he offered me the job. I was giddy as could be on the inside.

"So, how did it go?" Olivia appeared next to me and bumped into my shoulder with her elbow.

"I got the job. I start now, I guess."

"Awesome. I hoped ya would."

"Why's that? You don't even know me."

"I had a good feeling about ya." She grinned.

"Callie, can ya come back in about an hour? Olivia can train ya during lunch rush." Jesse handed me the shirts.

"Um . . ." I stammered. Training during a rush terrified me. "Sure. I'll go home and change. Thank you, Jesse. I truly appreciate it."

I drove back to the inn with a smirk glued to my face. I had never been a waitress before, but I was determined to make it work. It *had* to work. Excitement filled me as I couldn't wait to share the news with Marie and Carl. As the inn came into view, my smile faded quickly, fear piercing my heart. An ambulance was parked out front, lights flashing. Dread flooded through me. I ran inside to see Carl lying on a gurney. Marie was close behind.

"Marie, what happened?" I asked, laying my hand on Marie's forearm.

Marie's tears were heavily streaming down her cheeks. She muttered, "Carl . . . heart."

My heart broke for her, but she needed me to be strong in this moment as she was visibly falling apart. I inhaled deeply to help calm me and keep my composure. "You go with them, and I'll meet you at the hospital."

Marie swallowed hard as she nodded and followed the EMTs out the door. I ran up the stairs as fast as I could. Expecting it to be a long day at the hospital, I changed into some sweatpants and a T-shirt. Comfort would be needed. I thought about Carl, and a tear made its way down my cheek. Even though I had only met them a couple of days before, they already felt like family. I grabbed my bag and hurried out the door. Digging in my backpack, I found the map of the town I had gotten the day before.

I stood at the hospital's entrance, willing myself to step inside but wanting to run in the opposite direction. I needed to be there for Marie. I didn't know if she had anyone else. When I finally lifted my legs and stepped into the hospital, I went to the information desk. Someone called my name from behind me. I turned to see Marie looking frail. I went to her and wrapped my arms around her.

"They took him up to do scans and check his heart."

"Oh, Marie. I'm so sorry," I said, pulling out of the hug.

Marie sniffled. "They told me to stay here and that they'd come get me when they're done."

"I'll stay with you."

"Oh, but, Callie, you have other things to do today."

"None of which are more important than being here with you right now." I wasn't sure from where the comment came. My fondness for Marie and Carl had happened so fast. I had never experienced that before.

Marie held up her hand, but I shook my head. Her shoulders slumped, and she hugged me. "You're a sweet, sweet girl, Callie St. Claire."

I stepped back, searching out seats for us to sit in and wait, when a deep, familiar voice broke through the noisy waiting room.

"Aunt Marie, what happened?"

I glanced up to see Colt reaching out to Marie. *Aunt?* I had no idea I was staying with his aunt and uncle. When his eyes met mine, I would've loved to get lost in them. I forced my eyes away. My heart fluttered, and my knees wobbled. I didn't know what that meant, but I had to sit down.

"Callie, what are ya doin' here?"

"I got a job at the Bistro, and I went back to the inn to change and saw the ambulance. I couldn't *not* be here." At the mention of the Bistro, Colt's jaw clenched. *What was that about?* I wondered. Before I could dwell on it, I heard another familiar male voice.

"Mom, is Dad going to be okay?"

"Jesse?" I whispered under my breath.

Jesse gave Marie a long hug. I could see the fear and worry on his face.

"I don't know, sweetie. I'm waiting on the doctors to run their tests."

"Colt." Jesse's demeanor went from fear and worry to rigid with tension. "What are you doing here?"

"Jesse." Colt was just as short as he stuffed his hands in his front pockets. "This is my family. Of course, I'd be here." His jaw tightened with every word.

"Callie?" Jesse directed his attention to me when the air was filled with too much tension.

"Hey, Jesse," I greeted him quietly.

"What are you doing here?" he asked in a voice much harsher than what I had experienced earlier at the Bistro.

"I'm so sorry. I meant to call to say I needed to start tomorrow, but I wanted to get here so Marie wasn't alone . . ."

"How do you even know my mother?"

"I'm staying at the inn." I felt like a child being punished. "It appears she won't be alone now, so I'll just head back to the inn."

I made my exit while Marie was tracking down a doctor. I heard Colt and Jesse arguing semi-quietly as I scurried away. *They aren't my family. They aren't my family,* I repeated to myself as the tears began to fall from my eyes. I hated confrontation for obvious reasons. *Get yourself together, girl.*

Chapter 7

Colt

"**G**ood grief, Jesse. What's wrong with you?" I furrowed my brows.

"*Me?* What did *I* do?" Jesse tossed his hands in the air and then let them smack against his legs.

"Asked her what she was doing here like she did something wrong and isn't welcome."

"Well, she was supposed to be at the Bistro working, and we aren't her family. Heck, you are barely my family as far as I'm concerned."

I snickered. "The feeling's mutual."

"Where's Callie?" Aunt Marie asked as she wandered back to us. Her eyes darted from me to Jesse and back again. "Did you two run her off with your bickering? When are you two going to grow up and stop all this nonsense? One of you needs to fix this and fix it now." She huffed.

We knew she meant business. Aunt Marie was never one to mince words.

"Yes, ma'am," we both responded at the same time.

"I've got this." Jesse grinned at me.

"No!" I snapped and stopped him with my arm to his chest. "*I* got this."

I took off down the hall, peeking behind me to see if Jesse

would follow. Relief washed over me as I saw him staying with Aunt Marie. I had no idea if I would even find Callie or if she had left the hospital. I was relieved to find her sitting in a row of chairs by the entrance.

"Callie," I whispered, almost too low for her to hear.

"I just couldn't bring myself to leave. I know they aren't my family." The tears made their presence known in the corners of her eyes as her bottom lip quivered.

"Oh, Callie," I said softly as I enveloped her and folded her into my chest.

After the tears subsided, Callie pulled away. It took everything in me to keep from drawing her back in. I liked how she felt there.

"I'm sorry. That's the second time I've done that to you, Colt. I'm sure the last thing you need is some girl always crying on your shoulder." She tried to giggle.

"One thing you'll learn about me is that my shoulder is always open for anyone who needs it." When I peered into her eyes, I swore I saw fear, but it quickly vanished and was replaced by something else I couldn't quite pinpoint. She seemed empty somehow. I decided, then and there, I would do everything in my power to see her eyes sparkle, even if it was only for a moment.

"I should just go," Callie said.

"Aunt Marie wants ya here. *I* want ya here." The slightest hue of pink appeared on her cheeks with a hint of a smile. "Come on. Aunt Marie will kill me if I don't bring ya back." I nodded my head in the direction from which we had come.

I stood and held out my hand. I wasn't sure if she would take it or not, but I left it there. She bit her bottom lip, contemplating. She laid her hand in mine, and I pulled her up. I was happy when she didn't let go as we made our way back down the hall.

"There you are, sweet girl," Aunt Marie said, glaring at me and dragging Callie down to the seat next to her. "Don't you ever leave like that again."

"Yes, ma'am." Callie's chin fell to her chest. "Have you heard anything?"

Aunt Marie wrapped her arm around Callie's shoulder. "They said he had a mild heart attack. They want to keep him overnight for observation. I'm going to stay with him. Why don't you kids go back to the inn?" Aunt Marie placed her hand on Callie's cheek and gazed at her with such affection. I knew this was not a request but an order.

"How will you get home tomorrow? Do you need me to bring you anything?" Callie asked.

"No, dear. Jesse is going to get some of Carl's and my things and bring them here." She patted Callie's hand.

"Okay. Are you sure? Do you want me to stay until he gets back?"

"No, you go on ahead. Jesse told me to tell you to be at the Bistro tomorrow morning at ten to help prep for lunch if you're still interested in the job."

"Of course, I am."

At the mention of the Bistro and Jesse's name, I ground my teeth. The image of Callie working for and near him made my skin crawl. I couldn't help the low growl that escaped. Aunt Marie glared at me. I flashed her a sheepish grin and escorted Callie out of the hospital.

"I'll follow ya back to the inn," I told her when we reached her yellow Jeep. The thing looked ancient.

"You don't have to do that. I'll be fine on my own."

"I know I don't have to, but I also know you're the only guest at the inn right now, and I don't want ya to be there all alone."

"Okay." She gave in with a sigh.

I smirked as I closed her door. I was happy she didn't put up a fight.

Once we were back at the inn, I suggested, "Why don't ya go relax a little while I scrounge us up somethin' to eat?"

"That sounds nice. I guess I haven't had the chance to eat yet today except for a muffin this morning."

Callie disappeared up the stairs before I moved to the kitchen to forage for food. Rummaging through the refrigerator, I hoped to find something I could heat up. I was a master on the grill, but in the kitchen, I was definitely not. Leftover barbecue chicken and macaroni and cheese. Yes! Jackpot! Thank you, Aunt Marie. I found two plates and dished some food onto each before placing them in the oven to heat up.

I knew the second she stepped into the room. It wasn't because I heard her or caught a whiff of her scent. I couldn't explain it. It completely baffled me. I just felt her presence with every fiber of my being. It was like her soul was somehow connected to mine. It made goosebumps form all over my arms. When I turned around, I wasn't prepared for the vision before me. I didn't know how a woman with her hair pulled back, sweatpants on, and no makeup could take my breath away, but Callie succeeded. I found her absolutely stunning. She wasn't the type of woman every man would go ga-ga over. She wasn't the world's idea of what a beautiful woman was supposed to be, but I found her to be the perfect woman—for me. *Steady yourself, Colt. You don't even know her.*

I collected myself before I spoke. "I thought ya were gonna relax?" I raised a brow.

"I did. I took a shower. How much more relaxing can I do?"

"Lunch is almost ready. Why don't ya sit? I'll bring it out when it's done."

"Okay." Callie turned on her heel and left the kitchen.

I let out a breath I hadn't realized I was holding in. My head just wasn't clear when she was close. It had only been a day since I first saw her in the Bistro. She doesn't even know how beautiful she is, does she? *Get yourself together, Colt.* What has this woman done to me? I shrugged, took the plates out of the oven, and delivered them to the dining room table.

"Be careful. Plate is hot." I set one plate in front of her.

"Oh, barbecue chicken and mac and cheese." Callie inhaled as she closed her eyes.

"If ya don't like it, we can order pizza or something."

"No. This is one of my favorites." She beamed.

I sat across from her. "Mine, too. Do ya mind if I pray?"

"No, please do."

We held hands. I tried my hardest to ignore the spark I felt when our hands joined together.

"Lord, we ask that You bless this food to the nourishment of our bodies. Please watch over Uncle Carl and Aunt Marie. Help us to keep our focus on You so Your will can be done in our lives. In Jesus' name. Amen."

"Amen."

When Callie removed her hand from mine, she took the warmth with her. I shivered. Already, I thought if she disappeared from my life, I would be a shell of a man. I didn't understand it, but I knew it to be true.

"Are you not hungry?" Callie asked, taking me out of my head.

"Yeah, sorry." I coughed and lowered my head to hide my flushing cheeks.

I took my first bite. I could hear angels sing. I had forgotten Aunt Marie's cooking was so delicious. It had been too long. I made a mental note to visit them more often. We ate in what should have been an awkward silence, but somehow it felt so natural. After we finished, I picked up the dishes.

"I'll help you," Callie said, following me into the kitchen.

"Okay. I'll wash, you dry?" I glanced down at her.

"Sounds good." Callie grabbed a towel.

We kept things lighthearted, and I even managed to make her laugh a little. Her laugh was a beautiful sound. I hoped I could get her to laugh over and over again. It made me chuckle also. When the dishes were washed and put away, I laid the dishcloth over the faucet to dry, and Callie hung the towel on the oven door.

"Do you want to watch a movie?" I didn't want my time with her to end.

"Sure. What do you want to watch?"

Callie followed me to the common room, and we both sat on opposite ends of the couch at the same time. I desperately wanted to tell her she could sit closer, but I wasn't ready for her to leave me, and I felt if I asked her, that was exactly what she would do.

"Anything you've been wanting to see?" I asked her.

"Anything you pick is fine as long as it's not sci-fi or scary."

I picked up the remote and started flipping through movies. "How about this classic?"

My eyes made their way over to find Callie had fallen asleep. It had been a long and rough morning for her, I was sure. She really was a sight to behold. Pulling the throw blanket off the back of the couch, I gently covered her. I sat back on the couch, threw my arm over the back, and pushed play. I wasn't about to leave her there alone. But I soon found myself nodding off, and I didn't fight it. It had been a long morning for me also.

Chapter 8

Callie

I woke to a racing heart. I had no idea why it was about to pump out of my chest. How long had I been asleep? I rubbed my eyes to get them to focus before looking around the room, feeling a little disoriented. I forgot I was in the common room with Colt when I fell asleep. Darkness had descended on the room, and it took my vision a few minutes to adjust.

I sat up, expecting to be alone, but at the other end of the couch was a sleeping Colt. The sight of him sleeping made me feel warm inside. He could have left me alone, but he didn't. I recalled how my hand tingled when I placed it in his at lunch. His was calloused and a little rough. Those hands had worked hard. For some reason, I felt a sense of safety with him. I didn't understand it, but I felt it. It was something I hadn't had since my parents died. The emotion was comforting and terrifying all at the same time. It was comforting because, almost more than anything, I wanted to feel safe again. It was terrifying because it meant I would have to potentially open myself up to someone with the possibility of getting hurt.

I slowly moved from the couch to standing so I didn't disturb Colt. I glanced at the clock on the wall. One-thirty a.m. Had I really slept that long? I groaned because I had to get up early to go to my first day at the Bistro. I tiptoed up to my room and into the bathroom. I paused in front of the mirror. *You need to stop whatever you are feeling for Colt*, I told myself. Why would he be interested in me anyway? Look at me, with my wild, out-of-control, red hair and my 225-pound body. I rolled my eyes. The last thing I remembered was sitting on the bed.

My eyes popped open to my alarm blaring in my ear. I smacked the off button and let out a huge sigh. With all the sleep I had been getting, I should have been so much more rested. I guess I was sleeping so much because after spending the last fourteen years in survival mode, as my body unwound and felt safer, it needed more rest. I shrugged my shoulders and got up to get ready to go. I threw my hair up in a bun and went downstairs.

"Ready for your first day?" Colt asked

The sound of his voice almost gave me a heart attack. I didn't know he was still there. I placed my hand on my heart as if it would slow my heart rate.

"Sorry, I didn't mean to scare ya." He laughed.

"Just wasn't expecting you to be here."

"Oh." He slid a plate of pancakes over to me. "I told ya I wasn't going to leave ya here alone."

"What's this?" I asked, pointing to the plate.

"Most common folks call that there breakfast." He smirked, pointing to the plate. "Banana pancakes, in fact."

I stuck my tongue out at him in response. I took a bite. Wow! They were delicious. They were perfectly golden brown and fluffy. They melted as they touched my tongue. Perfect pancake to banana ratio. It had been forever since I'd had pancakes. My mom used to make them every Saturday. The memory made me smile and do a little wiggle in my seat.

"Mmm." My brows lifted in surprise.

"Surprised?" He chuckled.

I shrugged and took another bite. I concentrated on my chewing, making sure I didn't eat as if I had been starved for months. *Chew your food, Callie. Enjoy it. Don't make him think you're a total pig.* I peered at the clock and almost choked on the piece of pancake I was in the middle of chewing.

"Oh no! I thought I set my alarm for earlier than this. I'm going to be late. Thank you for breakfast. It was wonderful."

"Come to the ranch after work," Colt called after me.

"Okay."

I was perplexed by his asking me to the ranch again. Should I go or not? I grabbed my bag and keys and hurried out the door. After hopping in my Jeep, I headed down Broad Street to the Bistro—no time to walk like I had planned. When I arrived, I felt déjà vu as I took a deep breath and strode inside.

"Hey, Callie! So glad you're here. How's Carl?" Olivia greeted with a face of concern.

"Hey, Olivia. He had a mild heart attack. I haven't had the chance to talk with Marie yet this morning, but he is supposed to be able to come home today."

"That's so good to hear."

"Where can I put my stuff?"

"Follow me." She motioned with a wave of her hand.

"Thank you. So, what's first?" I asked, tying the black apron she had handed me around my waist. I slid my favorite pen into one of the pockets.

I spent the morning learning how to set up the tables, how to run the ordering and paying system, and the ins and outs of the kitchen.

"Obviously, you don't have to remember everything on your first day, but you need to learn quickly because it gets crazy around here, especially during lunch and supper." Olivia tried to reassure me. "You can just follow me around for a bit and observe. You can help me deliver food to tables, get drinks, and anything else. Then, maybe after the lunch rush, you can take some orders, and I can walk ya through the process. For now, though, why don't ya take your half-hour break because ya won't get one until after lunch."

"You don't have to tell me twice." I let out a hearty laugh.

I breathed a sigh of relief. I was a fast learner, but there was a lot to take in all at once. I hoped I could remember it and get it down fast. For my break, I decided to wander over to Courageous Café and Bakery again. I was going to need a sugar rush for what was to come. The bells jingled, signaling I had come through the door.

"Hi, Callie." Caitlyn offered the same bright grin she had the last time I was in. "What can I get for ya?"

"You remembered my name." I beamed.

I needed some comfort food and drink as I was totally out of my element at the Bistro and needed to calm my nerves. Food had always been my constant friend through everything. I supposed that was also why I was in this body. I ordered my hot chocolate and cupcake anyway. Both good to comfort and bring the sugar rush I was going to need.

"Have a seat, and I'll bring it over to ya."

"Thanks, Caitlyn."

Caitlyn gave me a big grin before disappearing to get my order ready. I sat at a table near the window. I loved sitting by the windows so I could watch the world go by and the people in it. Before long, Caitlyn brought my order out.

"Here ya go. Let me know if ya need anything else."

"Thanks. This looks yummy."

"No problem."

Caitlyn practically skipped to the back. She seemed like a very sweet girl. I hoped I could come to know her. Where did that come from? It caught me by surprise as I had been a loner type for so long. I never really had an interest in getting to know anyone. Maybe that was the start of something new. Before long, it was time to head back to the Bistro. I took a deep breath. *You can do this, Callie.*

Throughout the day, I followed Olivia around, making mental note of everything. I was going to have to write down as much as I could recall when I got back to my room. When the lunch rush was finally over, we both let out a deep sigh of relief.

"Wow! That was intense." I sighed with exhaustion as I plopped down in a nearby chair.

"Now, it's your turn to take some orders."

I wasn't too nervous until I saw the next patron walk through the door—Colt.

"Ah, your first customer." Olivia giggled as she retreated to the kitchen.

Don't leave me here alone, I wanted to shout. My hands began to sweat. *You got this, Callie.* I straightened my shoulders, ran my hands down my pants, and sashayed over to the table with as much confidence as I could curate.

"Good afternoon." I flashed a toothy grin at everyone at the table.

"Afternoon, Callie," Colt responded. He locked eyes with me for a little longer than I was comfortable with, and it made my heart do a flip-flop.

"Can I start you off with something to drink, or are you ready to order?"

"I'll have a water and club sandwich with fries."

"I'll get these in for you," I said after taking everyone's

orders.

"Thank ya."

"Well, ya got your first order in," Olivia stated like a proud parent as I entered the kitchen through the swinging doors.

"Yep." I exhaled deeply.

I filled up the water glass for Colt, the sodas for the others, and did my best to balance the tray while I slowly returned to their table. I set the tray on the table across from them, and as I turned to set Colt's water glass on the table, my hand collided with his. I gasped, and my eyes widened, the cup seeming to fall in slow motion. The water hit his thigh, and the cup landed with a thud on the floor.

"I'm so sorry, Colt." Panic bubbled up from my toes to the rest of my body.

I grabbed some napkins to clean up the mess I had caused. Before my hand could reach his pants, he seized hold of my wrist.

"I got it." His voice sounded pained.

His eyes swirled like a burning fire and confused me. Was he mad at me? Was it something else? I ran to the back before anyone could see the first tear fall.

"Callie, what happened?" Jesse asked as he strode over to me from the office. He must have heard my body collide with the swinging doors.

"Nothing." I wiped my eyes before turning around to face him. "I'm sorry. I don't usually react this way. I guess I'm more frustrated with myself than anything."

"Tell me what happened."

"I spilled water on Colt, and he got mad."

Jesse stifled a chuckle and wrapped his arms around me. "It'll be okay. I'm sure he wasn't mad."

Jesse's arms around me felt so different than Colt's. It gave

51

me shivers. I shook it off and chalked it up to Jesse being my boss. I wasn't the type of girl to mess around personally with my boss. I shied away from his hug as quickly as I could.

"Thank you." I sniffled.

"For what?" he asked as he gently tucked my hair behind my ear.

"For the hug. For not getting angry with me and yelling at me." I stared at my hands interlocked at the bottom of my stomach.

"Oh, Callie. What have people done to you?" he asked softly.

I gazed up at him, smiled slightly, and shrugged.

He tried to hug me once more. I put my hand against his chest. "Thank you. I'm okay now."

Chapter 9

Colt

"**C**olt!" Olivia yelled as she stared me down.

"What?" I snapped back. I was used to Olivia scolding me. She had done it since we were kids.

"Ya didn't have to be so rude." She stuck her fists on her hips.

"I wasn't tryin' ta be." I sighed as I pressed my palms into my eyes and rubbed them back and forth.

"Well, why is she crying then? It was an accident." Olivia threw her hands up.

"I know that." I growled. "I just couldn't let her touch me." My physical reaction to Callie was unlike anything I had ever experienced. I couldn't let myself lose control.

I peered up at Olivia, hoping she would take the hint. By her expression, it seemed as if she did.

"Oh," she said, "oooooh."

"Yeah." I sighed.

"Well, then, go after her." She motioned to the kitchen.

I stood and all but ran in the direction Callie had gone. I didn't get far before my feet were frozen where they were planted. I clenched my jaw and fists, and my nostrils flared. My eyes started to sting.

What I saw through the windows of the kitchen doors was

something I was used to, but I had hoped Callie was different. I had a connection with her, and I was certain she felt it, too. She had to. My body tensed as Jesse tucked Callie's hair behind her ear and pulled her into his arms. I didn't stick around to watch. This time, instead of making things worse, I went back to the table and slapped money down. I had to get out of there.

"I've lost my appetite," I told Olivia as I shoved open the door so hard it banged against the building.

"Colt! What happened?" Olivia called after me, but I was too angry to stick around.

Jesse had done this kind of thing our entire lives. He would find out I wanted something, and he would receive it and then rub my nose in it. He did the same with women. It hadn't happened in about four years. Not since Julia. She had been my steady girlfriend since high school. When my dad passed and my mom left, I guess I became distant, and that's when Jesse swooped in. I was going to ask her to marry me, but she chose him instead. She left town not long after.

I hadn't been interested in anyone since Julia, so Jesse hadn't had the opportunity until now. After Julia, I'd sworn off women and concentrated on getting Redemption Ranch up and running. I re-dedicated my life to Christ and never glanced back. That's why I couldn't let Callie touch me. Not until I felt on more solid ground. I was too afraid to lose sight of keeping Christ at the center. If Callie wasn't who God had for me, then I didn't want to do anything to mess up what He did have for me. The more I thought about Jesse, the more I wanted to punch something—no, some*one*. But I was better off going home and taking a ride instead. It was safer for everyone that way.

Once back at the ranch, I saddled up Beauty and headed out. I had named her that because she resembled the horse from the books and movies, except her white mark was in the shape of a heart. Remembering when Dad gave her to me brought a grin to my face. I had just turned eighteen and had graduated high school a few months before. He told me, "Son, you're an adult now, and if you're gonna take over the ranch one day, ya need your own horse."

Over the next few years, my dad taught me everything I needed to know about running the ranch. It had been the best time of my life because I got to spend so much time with him. That time was the only consolation after he died. I cherished those memories because that was all I had left. At first, I didn't really know why I felt a connection to Callie, but maybe our losses were what drew me to her. She understood my pain like no one else I knew—not even Jon. His loss was a different kind. But that isn't my story to tell.

Beauty had become one of my best friends, maybe even the best. She knew all of my thoughts, dreams, and desires. She knew things I couldn't tell anyone else. Jon didn't even know everything that my horse did. When we reached the creek that ran through the ranch, I let Beauty drink and rest. I sat beneath my favorite tree. It was my favorite because my mom, dad, and I planted it together. I bowed my head and did what I found myself doing more and more each day. I prayed.

"God help me! Help me to keep my cool with Jesse. If Callie is supposed to be with him, show me. I will love, honor, and glorify You whether Callie is meant to be in my life romantically or as just a friend. I don't want anything that isn't of Your will. Guide me, Lord. Amen."

I sat with my eyes closed, being still, waiting for God to speak to me if He chose. I grew up in a Christian family, but when my dad died and my mom moved, I became angry with Him. Especially after Julia left. In getting my life back with

Christ at the center, I learned Julia and I didn't have a relationship that was right in the eyes of God. I truly believed that was why our relationship ended without much of a fight. I needed something to ground me, so I re-dedicated my life to Him. I had been doing everything within my power to live right by Him. I didn't want to be like others I had seen who lost control when people had left, either by death or just leaving.

Go home. I heard as plain as day from out of nowhere. My eyes darted around because the voice seemed so close and real, but I only found myself alone. I stood and took hold of Beauty's reins.

"Ya ready to go back, girl?"

Beauty whinnied as I climbed on. I wanted to stretch her legs on the way back, so we galloped to the stable. I loved the feel of the wind on my face when we were moving so fast. It was exhilarating and freeing. As we approached the stable, my heart nearly stopped. The old yellow Jeep was parked outside. I jumped down and guided Beauty into the stable.

"Callie," I was barely able to get out due to my heart being caught in my throat at the sight of her standing there . . . on my property. "What're ya doin' here?"

Callie turned around with sadness in her eyes. They appeared glassy and red as if she had been crying. "You left without your food. Why did you leave? Is it because I spilled water on you?" She extended a take-home bag.

"After ya ran off, I went searching for ya. I saw ya with Jesse. Ya need to know he's just using ya to get to me." I stood staring into her eyes with my hands on my waist. Callie's body stiffened, and her jaw set as she dropped the bag to the ground. I should have said that differently.

"Why? Because a man would never be interested in a woman like me? Because I'm not worth a man's time or attention?" Tears formed in her eyes as she whipped around, turning her back to me. "Maybe coming here was a mistake," she muttered.

"Callie." I sighed and caught her wrist. "Please look at me."

She slowly twirled and faced me. I was screwing this up. *Lord, help me.* I did the most desperate thing ever. I drew her close to me and kissed her. Her lips were unlike anything I had ever experienced. I released her wrist, ran my fingertips up her arms, and cupped her face in my hands. Fireworks exploded inside me as I sensed a sudden warmth from my head to my toes. The heavens opened, and God, Himself, was shining down on us.

When I broke the kiss, it was all too soon, but we were both breathless. I opened my eyes and couldn't decipher the expression on Callie's face. Was it horror? Surprise? Whatever it was, she didn't say a word. Not. A. Single. Word. Not the response I had hoped for. She bolted out the door, and I couldn't do anything to stop her. So much for following my heart. I ran my hand through my hair and let out a breath. I could stand there and try and figure women out, or I could bury myself in work and try and forget about her. I growled and headed for the stalls.

Chapter 10

Callie

I ran as fast as I could back to my Jeep. I jumped in and sped away. My heart was racing, and my lungs couldn't expand enough for me to catch my breath. What just happened? I touched my still-tingling lips. No man had ever kissed me like that before—like he meant it. Ever. A frustrated growl escaped. *Why did he do that? He basically told me Jesse didn't want me because* . . . I couldn't bring myself to finish that thought. I wished I had more experience with the opposite sex. My aunt's voice swirled in my head, telling me I would never be good enough. Confusion flooded me. No point in fretting over him or that perfect, wonderful kiss. Would I ever understand men? I shook my head, turned up the radio, and drove back to the inn.

Once inside, something clanged in the kitchen, but I didn't feel like chatting with anyone, so I hustled upstairs to take a shower and then to read the book I had checked out from the library. As I settled on the bed and grabbed my book from the nightstand, a knock came to the door. I ran my fingers through my hair just in case it was Colt.

"Come in."

Marie poked her head in the door. "Are you okay, dear? I heard you come in, but you didn't come say hello like you usually do."

I tried to hide my disappointment with a grin. "I'm fine. I just got this book at the library, and I couldn't wait to read it."

Marie glanced from the book to me. "Well, holler if you need anything."

"I will. Thank you."

Marie closed the door, and I opened my book. It was one of the Alex Cross series books by James Patterson. Typically, I would have selected a book by Karen Kingsbury, but a love story was the last thing I needed. They always caused an ache in the middle of my chest and made me long for what may never be. No, what I needed was a good suspenseful murder mystery. I always got drawn into the hunt for the murderer, as well as the mindset of that character and Alex Cross. What would it be like to be a forensic psychologist, trying to get into the minds of murderers and serial killers? After a few pages, the words began to blur, and my eyelids grew heavy.

"I love you, Callie," he confessed so softly I wondered if I'd heard him correctly. His thumb lightly cascaded down my cheek, leaving a tingling sensation in its wake.

"Please don't say that." My cheeks became warm as I glanced down at my clasped hands.

"Why not?" His voice broke as his hand fell back to his side.

My voice quivered. "Because you don't mean it. Men never do."

He stepped closer and placed his fingers under my chin and lifted my head. He pressed his lips ever so gently to mine and deepened the kiss only when I didn't pull away. I was cemented in place. The kiss lasted mere seconds but felt like a lifetime. "Now tell me I don't mean it," he whispered breathlessly as he leaned his forehead to mine.

I shot straight up in bed. My heart was racing a mile a minute, and my lips were tingling just like they had after Colt kissed me in the stable. His kiss in my dream was just as powerful. It wasn't the kiss I was truly thinking about, though. I heard those words echo in my head. Men had said those things to me before, but not even one of them meant it. They said it to get what they wanted before disappearing from my life.

A tear rolled down my cheek. I swiped it away as if someone might see. I decided I needed to steer clear of Colt until I could get my feelings under control, or at least my expectations. I turned over in bed and went back to sleep, praying Colt wouldn't make an appearance again.

Chapter 11

Colt

I arose early to get started on the day. I hadn't had time to dwell on the fact I had kissed Callie. I had already berated myself, so there was nothing else I could do about it. My night had been spent rescuing a young horse from the woods. I had been awakened in the middle of the night by an anonymous caller. I grabbed Jon, and we headed to where the caller told me the colt was located. When I saw the horse, I knew he wasn't in good shape. I wasn't certain of the extent of his injuries since it was pitch black in the middle of the woods, but I knew he wouldn't survive there. It took everything Jon and I had to get him in the trailer. I apologized profusely over and over again for any pain we may have caused him, but when we finally got him in the trailer, he seemed to settle a little.

"How's he doin' today?" Jon interrupted my thoughts.

"He seems to be doin' a little better. Still can't get him to eat. Doc Norris is coming later to take a look at him. He also won't let anyone touch him much, but I can't blame him there."

"That's good. Doc will get ya fixed right up, buddy," Jon told the colt as he ran his hand up and down the colt's nose. It wasn't long before the colt moved his head out of Jon's reach. "Any luck with a name?" He leaned against the beam that separated the stall gates and crossed his arms.

"I think we'll call him Warrior," I informed Jon over my shoulder as I filled up a bucket with water and placed it in the stall.

Warrior had been beaten with a whip on more than one occasion. It made my blood boil. I couldn't understand how anyone could treat an animal that way. I knew people in the racing world started training colts at about ten months of age. I couldn't even imagine what Warrior had been through in his short time on Earth. He wouldn't let anyone touch him for long periods of time without getting anxious. I worried Doc Norris wouldn't be able to examine him properly.

"Colt," Doc Norris greeted as he stepped into the stable.

"Hey, Doc. Thanks for comin'. How are ya?" I shook his outstretched hand.

"Good. Good. Where's this poor fella at?"

"Warrior's over here." I nodded toward his stall. "It looks like he's got wounds in various stages of healin'. Looks like they're from a whip." My face grew hot with anger.

"Those racing people make me so angry sometimes." Doc growled.

"He will only let anyone touch his nose and not for an extended period of time."

"I can't say I blame him. Let's see what we can get done, shall we?" Doc moved closer to Warrior. "It's okay, boy." His voice was soft and calm.

Warrior startled a little before settling down. Doc went to examine one of the open wounds, and Warrior reared up. Doc barely made it out of the stall before Warrior stomped down where Doc had been standing.

"Whoa, boy!" I raised my hands in front of Warrior's face.

"That was close." Doc composed himself. "I think that's

enough for today. I'll give you some antibiotics and painkillers to help until I can come back and examine him some more. I'll give him some time to rest. Call the office and make an appointment for next week. Be sure to give him a painkiller an hour or so before. That might help."

"Okay. Great." I followed him out to his truck.

I didn't know if Warrior could be tamed and learn to trust me. Warrior reminded me a little of Callie. I didn't know if she would grow to trust me either. What happened to her? Had someone hurt her? I didn't know for sure, but I knew I would do everything I could to convince them both they could trust me.

Chapter 12

Callie

I had no idea what I was doing. I said I was going to avoid Colt until I could get my feelings under control. Yet, there I was, parking my Jeep outside his stable. The morning sun was still rising. I tried my best to look cute, though. I braided my hair over to the side, and I wore boots with jeans and a plaid, button-down shirt. I strode inside to find no one in sight. It was quiet. The place smelled of manure and fresh-cut hay. My eyes were immediately drawn to the sandy-colored horse with a white mane. I peered into his eyes as he stared back at me. I stepped closer, and I felt as if his gaze reached my soul. He snorted through his nostrils as he raised his head slightly.

"It's okay, boy." My voice remained gentle.

I raised my hand to show him I wasn't going to hurt him. The horse lowered his head and allowed me to pet him. He snorted as he moved his head to snuggle me. I continued to run my hands on his nose and the sides of his head.

"What did they do to you? Looks like you have some scarring, too." I talked to him as I ran my hand along his side as far as I could reach, which wasn't far. Thank you, short arms and legs. I rolled my eyes. I was careful not to touch any wounds or scars.

He whinnied. I looked around, and when I saw I was alone,

I opened the stall gate and slipped inside.

"You're safe now. No one is going to hurt you anymore. Colt will take good care of you. He'll make sure you feel safe. He has a way of doing that. I just met him, and he makes me feel safe for the first time since . . ." I couldn't finish the sentence. "It also terrifies me. I learned a long time ago you just can't trust people, but something in me trusts him. You can trust him, too."

Chapter 13

Colt

As I rounded the corner into the stable, a voice emitted from Warrior's stall. Callie? I must be hearing things. The wind picked up, whistling through the leaves that surrounded the ranch. But then I heard it again. Definitely Callie. What was she doing here? I hurried to the stall to warn her, but when she came into view, Warrior was allowing her to touch him. I knew I shouldn't have eavesdropped, but I wanted to be close enough to pull her away if Warrior reared up again. I peered through a small crack in the wall so I could stay out of sight.

"I have scars, too. See?" She lifted her shirt to show Warrior her back.

I could hear the pain in her voice. I wanted to go to her, to comfort her, but I didn't want to ruin the moment she was having with the horse. Warrior hadn't let anyone touch him like he was letting her. This led me to believe those wounds were at the hands of a man.

"I'd better go. I'll come back and see you again. Be a good boy." She kissed him, and Warrior neighed in response. The stall gate opened, and Callie appeared.

"Callie," I said softly for fear of startling her.

She jumped and whirled around. Her cheeks became rosy. "Colt," she responded, her hand over her heart. "How long have you been standing there?"

I wanted to lie—to tell her I had just arrived—but I knew better than to think a relationship could be built on lies—even if they were white ones. "Long enough." I wanted her to show me what she had shown Warrior, but I didn't dare ask. I'd let her tell me in her own time. If that time ever came.

I wanted to have a serious discussion with Callie about going into a horse's stall without knowledge of its temperament, but I thought better of it. That would be a discussion for later— *if* we had a later. I motioned to Warrior. "He hasn't let anyone touch him like that, not even Doc Norris."

Callie bit her lip and confessed so low I could barely hear her. "Maybe it's because I understand his pain." She looked down at her feet and then back up at me. Tears shimmered in her eyes. I wanted to ask again but knew that was a story for another time.

"Ya want to help give him some medicine?"

"I'd like that very much." She grinned slightly.

So would I, I thought. "Put out your hand." I put some grain in her outstretched hand and buried the pills.

"Hey, boy," she said, placing her hand to his mouth. "You want some food?" Warrior turned his nose up like a defiant toddler. "Come on, boy. It will make you feel better. You have to eat, sweetness. It won't hurt you. I promise." It was as if he understood her promise because he stuck out his tongue and swiped up what was in her hand. "Good boy!" Callie flashed a grin that went from ear to ear. I could only dream of making her lips turn up like that. Warmth invaded me at the thought. "So, does he have a name?" She rubbed Warrior's nose.

"Warrior."

"That suits you, Warrior."

"It really does. I have no idea how people can be so cruel."

"I wish *I* didn't," Callie mumbled.

Those four little words broke my heart. I couldn't take it any longer, so I stepped closer and enveloped her in my arms. "I wish I could erase your pain, but I can't. All I can do is try and make your present and future better, if ya let me."

Callie wrapped her arms around me and held on tightly. I liked the way she felt in my arms, especially when she was hugging me back. She felt soft. She felt like home. She felt like in my arms was where she was meant to be. I wondered if she felt it, too. I wanted so badly to know, but I didn't dare ask.

"Ya know ya always have a place here, Callie," I whispered.

"I do? You mean Edenton?" she asked, leaving my arms.

"No." I sighed. "At Redemption Ranch . . . with me." I shoved my hands in my pockets. I didn't know what else to do with them. Why did I say that? "There's an open cabin. It's yours if ya want it. You'll have to work on the ranch at least ten hours a week in exchange. You could help with Warrior." I felt almost like a kid asking my parents for something I really wanted, hoping, praying they'd say yes.

Callie's eyes sparkled for just a moment. "Really?"

"Yes." I tried my best to convince her.

"I'd love that! Thank you, Colt!"

I stumbled backward as she launched herself into my arms, causing me to chuckle. "Are you working today?"

"No." She sighed. "Jesse had to let me go. He said I was lucky I spilled something on you and not someone else. He said I was a liability or something like that. I was struggling to learn everything anyway. It's okay. He found someone else that was catching on much quicker than me. I'm not cut out to be a waitress anyway. Besides, who wants to get their food from a fat girl?"

I huffed. "You are not fat. You are beautiful."

Callie's entire neck streaked red before slowly moving to her cheeks. It made me grin. I liked doing that to her. It seemed to be so easy to do. I hoped to do it more.

She averted her gaze and lowered her head, her tone low and unsure. "Thank you."

"Why don't ya come back tomorrow with your things, and I'll show ya the cabin. I'll give ya a tour of the ranch, too if ya'd like. There'll be plenty to do to get ready for the Fall Harvest Festival also."

"Festival?"

"Yeah, we started it here at the ranch a few years ago. We have vendors, contests, hayrides, and other things. There's also a dance the last night." At that moment, I imagined her in my arms, slow dancing to every song.

"Oh, I've never been to a festival like that. I'd love to help. It will help keep my mind off the upcoming anniversary."

"It must be hard that it's your birthday, too. When was the last time ya felt special on that day?"

"It was a month before my sixteenth birthday. They had given me the Jeep." She pointed toward the door with her thumb over her shoulder before interlacing her hands and staring down at the ground.

So, *that's* why she drove that old thing. I didn't know what to say. However, my mind began going wild with ideas, especially since she would be at the ranch.

"I'd better get going so I can pack my stuff and say goodbye to Marie and Carl."

"Well, it's not really goodbye. It really is a small town." I smirked.

"So, I'll see you tomorrow?" She tilted her head to the side and glanced up at me.

"Yep. Just come out whenever you're ready." I grinned

like a little schoolboy to his crush.

"Can I ask you a question?" She bit her bottom lip.

"Sure. Anything."

"The last time I was here, you said Jesse was just using me to get to you, as if he wouldn't go for a fat girl like me . . ." she trailed off.

"Callie, that's not what I meant at all. I'm so sorry. I wish ya could see yourself the way I see ya. You're a beautiful woman. Don't let anyone ever tell ya different."

Her bottom lip stuck out farther than her top one. "Then what did you mean?"

I sighed. I didn't want to tell her I wanted her, but I didn't know how to explain what Jesse had always done without confessing. "Jesse has just always been very competitive with me."

"Okay." She seemed to accept my explanation. I breathed a sigh of relief. "Just so you know, I didn't let him hug me again. He hugged me once, and it made me uncomfortable. I guess you missed that part. See you tomorrow," she said before coming closer and kissing my cheek. She then strutted out of the stable.

I had no idea why I always suddenly felt empty when she left, but I did. She pushed him away? I wish I would have stuck around for that. She didn't choose Jesse. That made my heart skip a beat and brought a satisfied smile to my face.

"Guess I'd better go make sure the cabin is ready for tomorrow, Warrior." I looked over at him. "She's coming to live here." I was giddy inside.

I couldn't believe I invited Callie to live at the ranch. I had made it a no-woman zone long ago when Julia left me, but there was something super special about Callie. What would the guys think about her living on the ranch? Her innocent kiss rushed back to the forefront of my mind. I touched my cheek and couldn't help but grin. I made up my mind that she would be mine one day. By the grace of God, I would do everything in my power to make it happen.

Chapter 14

Callie

I couldn't believe I was moving to Redemption Ranch. My feelings for Colt were still under review as to what I was going to do with them. They'd have to stay hidden. With the front of my hair pulled back and the rest flowing down my back, I ran extra anti-frizz serum into it and added a little lip gloss to my usual makeup regimen of foundation and mascara. I slid into a pair of jeans and a black tank top, and I slipped on a short-sleeve, button-down plaid shirt, which I left open. Boots were added to the ensemble. I hoped I didn't look like I was trying too hard. I packed the rest of my things and headed downstairs.

Marie, Carl, and I said our goodbyes the night before, but I couldn't leave without giving them each a hug. I had mixed emotions. I was super excited to work with Warrior and, of course, Colt, but I was going to miss seeing Marie and Carl every day. I had only been staying with them for a few days, but it made me feel as if I'd had my parents back, just different people—if that made any sense at all. They made me feel like family since my first day there, and it made me feel as if part of me was starting to heal.

"Oh, good morning, Callie," Marie said, turning from the stove.

It smelled as if Marie was getting a head start on lunch as I knew breakfast had been over since 9 a.m., and it was 10:30. I couldn't pinpoint exactly what she was cooking as it wasn't a familiar scent, which made sense because my culinary skills were reduced to frozen dinners and take-out. I could only manage a slight smirk. I wanted to cry. Leaving Carl and Marie was close to the same emotions of losing my parents even though I would still see Carl and Marie from time to time. The way they interacted with each other and with me reminded me so much of my mom and dad. It was a feeling I wanted to hold on to forever.

"Oh, now. Don't be sad," Marie comforted me. "You have to move on to new adventures. This adventure sounds fun."

"I know. I'm just going to miss seeing you both every day." I swallowed hard and swiped at the tear that fell from my eye.

"Sweetie, you're family now. We will see each other often, and you can stop by any time you like." Marie came around the island and gave me a hug.

"Aww. Giving away hugs without me?" Carl pretended to be sad just before he wrapped his arms around both of us.

"Thank you for everything you've done for me. It has been so nice feeling like I have a family again."

"That's because you *do* have a family here," Carl said matter-of-factly.

"Okay. I guess I should get going. I will have so much to do to get settled and be able to help with Warrior. Wish me luck."

I had spent much of the previous evening talking with Marie and Carl about Warrior and how I was the only one he would let touch him. Every time I mentioned Colt's name, though, I saw Carl and Marie share a glance. I wasn't sure what that was about. Would I eventually find out? I shrugged.

73

"See you later, sweetie. Good luck!" Marie waved after me.

I grabbed the last of my things and practically skipped out to my Jeep. Carl and Marie had helped me pack my Jeep the night before. As I stepped up to slide into the driver's seat, I lovingly glanced back at the place that quickly became my home over the last week. When I had arrived in Edenton on that beautiful June morning, I had no idea I would find what I had been longing for—a place to call home—let alone so quickly. I took a deep breath, slid into the seat, and closed the door. I was ready for my new chapter at Redemption Ranch. For the first time in a long time, I was excited to see what would unfold. I wiggled in my seat before driving away.

As I pulled up to the stable, Colt came outside. He was the most beautiful man I had ever laid eyes on. He wasn't only beautiful on the outside; he was a great man on the inside as well—a man that made me dream of things I had no business dreaming. But what if he was in God's will for my life? I had no idea where that question came from. As soon as it left, I heard my aunt's voice once again. *Stupid Girl, look at him and look at you. A man like that could have any woman he wanted. Why in the world would he choose you?* I shook the voice from my head and strode over to Colt.

"Hey." I beamed up at him.

"Hey there."

Seeing him made my heart flutter. My palms became clammy. Those steel-blue eyes never ceased to take my breath away. His black hair was mussed from what I assumed was his morning chores.

"Do ya want to come say hi to Warrior before we head over to the cabins?" he asked, motioning toward the stable. He took a bandana out of his back pocket and wiped his hands and brow.

"I'd love to. How's he doing today?"

"Seems to be the same. I'm hoping having ya here will help him."

I hoped I could help. I hoped my being there helped me, too. I followed Colt inside. The thought that I could make a difference in Warrior's life made my heart sing. When I fixed my eyes on him, he whinnied as if he noticed me in the same moment.

Colt grinned. "He doesn't react to anyone the way he reacts to you. It's pretty amazing to witness, actually."

I peered up at Colt before walking over to greet Warrior. "Hey, boy. Did you miss me?" I asked, running my hand down his nose. "You're such a good boy, aren't you?" I kissed the side of his head. "I'll come back and see you later, okay?" Warrior snorted like he understood. I turned back to Colt. "Okay. I'm ready."

"Let me grab my truck, and you can follow me."

"Okay." I followed him outside, sizing him up from his heels to his head.

When I parked in front of the cabin that was to be my new home, I swallowed a lump that had taken up residence in my throat. It was perfect. I already felt like I was home. I wondered how much of that had to do with the cabin and how much had to do with the man standing in front of it, his eyes transfixed on me.

"It's not much, but this is it." Colt pointed to the cabin as I came to stand by him.

"Are you kidding me? It's perfect." I beamed.

"Let me help you bring your bags inside," he insisted, grabbing the bags I had set on the porch.

"I can get them," I offered. Colt didn't say a word. He just unlocked the door and strutted inside. "Well, okay then," I muttered.

After all my bags were inside the cabin, Colt turned toward the door. "Well, I'll leave ya ta get settled."

"Okay. Should I just come to the stable when I'm done?"

"If ya'd like." He rocked back on his heels, a sly grin rising on one side, a dimple making its presence known.

How had I missed that dimple before? You bet your boots I'd like to! I could feel my insides heating up, and it took everything I had to keep from shouting it. I coughed. "I would. Very much so."

"Okay. I'll see ya at the stable then."

"Okay." I watched him turn to go. "Hey, Colt?"

"Yeah?" He turned and faced me.

"Thank you so much." I smiled again.

"You're welcome." He winked and tipped his hat before getting in his truck and driving away.

This was the cutest place I had ever seen. The small porch had two rocking chairs. I couldn't wait to sit out there if I woke up early enough to enjoy the silence of the morning. The cabin resembled the cabins I used to build out of Lincoln Logs when I was a little girl. Inside, to the left, there was a small kitchen with a stove, a mini-fridge, some cabinets, and a rustic round wooden table with two chairs. I made a mental note I would need to buy some groceries. I found a few dishes in the cabinets.

On the right side of the cabin was the living room, complete with a love seat, recliner, solid wood coffee table, floor lamp, and a small TV hung on the wall above the mantle of a fireplace. Down the hall, I peeked into the bathroom. Nothing special there—just a toilet, a small vanity and mirror, and a shower—but I loved it all the same. I continued my trek down the hall. At the end was the bedroom. A queen-size, four-poster bed took up the far corner. Along the opposite wall were a dresser and mirror. I loved every inch of the cabin. I was a simple woman and didn't need much to make me happy, just a place to call home. I couldn't wait to make it my own. I needed to make a list of things I would need to buy—a comforter, pillows, and bath towels and mats, to name a few.

I drew the curtains, opened the window, and stared out at the expanse that was Redemption Ranch. I inhaled deeply to take in the mixture of red maple and oak with a faint scent of magnolia. I knew about the trees because it was part of my research about the area prior to moving. As I took in the splendor of the land, I jumped at a knock at the door. I opened the door expecting to see Colt, but instead, standing before me was Jon.

"Hi, Jon." I tried my best to mask my disappointment.

"Hey, Callie. I just wanted to welcome ya to the ranch and let ya know I'm right across the way if ya need anything." He motioned to the cabin directly behind him.

"Oh, well, thank you. So very nice of you." I smiled.

Awkward silence filled the space between us. Jon shoved his hands in his pockets.

"Well, I'll let ya get back to settlin' in. Nice to have ya here." He put his finger to the brim of his hat and nodded.

"Thank you, Jon. I'll see you later." I giggled as I closed the door, grabbed the bags I had left there, and went back to the bedroom. I knew I was going to love it there.

When I was done unpacking, exhaustion almost overtook me. I, again, thought maybe it was all the years of never feeling I was where I was supposed to be, so now that I felt home, I could take a breath. Maybe the sleep was my body's way of rejuvenating after all these years. I laid down on the bed, only intending to rest my eyes for a few minutes.

Thoughts of Colt swirled in my mind. He really was an amazing man. I couldn't understand why he was still single. My aunt's voice was right; he could truly have any woman he wanted. Did I really stand a chance? I'd better get my feelings in check and fast. There really was only one outcome for me—being hurt and disappointed. My thoughts finally dissipated as I grabbed the throw blanket that was spread out at the foot of the bed, squeezing it, wishing it was Colt. But my aunt's voice returned to my head, and with it, brought doubts. I punched the mattress and screamed into the blanket.

Chapter 15

Colt

I spent the afternoon feeding the horses, mucking out stalls, and thinking about Callie. I couldn't believe she was at the ranch, possibly for good, or so I hoped. So, why hadn't she come to the stable to see Warrior? I lugged a bale of hay and flopped it on the stack at the back of the stable and paced. Too bad she wasn't coming to see me. As if Warrior could read my thoughts, he neighed. I chuckled. How could I ever compare to the majestic Warrior?

I drove to the cabins, even though I could have walked up the road. I rolled down my window as it was a beautiful afternoon. The birds were chirping. There was a slight breeze that caused the aroma of the magnolia trees to waft into the cab of the truck. I parked in front of Callie's cabin and sauntered up to the door. I knocked, and it crept open. I sighed. I'd have to have a talk with her about making sure the door was closed tightly. Raccoons have been known to push open the doors and rummage through anything they could find, leaving a rubble of destruction in their path.

"Callie," I called out softly. I passed through the kitchen and living room with no sign of her. I continued to call out to her as I strode toward the back of the cabin. I glanced into the bathroom to find it unoccupied. Entering the doorway of the bedroom, I found Callie curled up in a ball on the bed. I smirked, crossed my arms, and leaned against the door jamb. For a minute, I allowed myself to wonder what it would be like to watch her sleep in my bed as my wife. She looked like an angel. I wanted her to be *my* angel.

Snap out of it, Colt. You just met her. Quit being a creeper. I shook my head and stepped over to the bed. "Callie, sweetheart," I said softly as I ran my fingers down her arm to try to rouse her. I didn't want to scare the living daylights out of her. "It's almost time for supper."

A small grin formed on her lips. Her eyes started to flutter open. "Hi," she said softly as her lips turned upward again. "What time is it?"

"Almost six o'clock."

Callie shot up. "What? No! I didn't mean to fall asleep. I missed working with Warrior." Her mouth formed a pout.

I laid my hand on hers and felt the spark radiate up my arm. Did she feel it, too? "Callie, it's okay. There'll be plenty of time for that. Ya just got here."

"I know, but I still need to pull my own weight."

Her hair was a tousled mess, but she never looked more beautiful. I held in a chuckle. This wasn't the time for her to think I was laughing at her. She was definitely eager and had a good work ethic. I valued those things in a person. Knowing that made me like her even more, if that was even possible.

"No one expects that today, okay?" Her shoulders lowered as she exhaled. "Why don't ya get washed up, and I'll meet ya outside?" I motioned toward the door with my thumb over my shoulder.

Callie glanced down at her clothes and ran her fingers through her hair. She peered at me with confusion stamped on her brow. "What's wrong with what I have on?" She wore a slight pout.

"I just thought ya might want to freshen up since you've been asleep is all."

"Oh. Okay," she responded, sliding off the bed.

It was in that instant my heart completely melted, and I knew I was a goner. I knew there would never be another woman for me . . . just her. I stepped out of the room and straight out the front door. While I stood outside, I took a deep breath and massaged my still-tingling hand. I had to slow my heart and my feelings down. I knew if I moved too fast with her, she'd run as fast as she could.

It wasn't long before Callie opened the door and joined me on the porch. I glanced at her out of the corner of my eye. She had pulled her hair back in a low ponytail and applied a little bit of clear lip gloss to her lips. She had also changed clothes. She wore a long shirt and black leggings with slip-on flat dress shoes.

"I'm ready."

"We typically have supper at my house. Is that okay? Or I can take ya somewhere if you'd rather."

"No. Whatever you normally do is fine with me."

"Let's go then. I can introduce ya to everyone."

"Perfect," she stated as she sucked her bottom lip between her teeth.

We jumped into my truck and rode down the winding dirt road to my house. I knew Callie hadn't seen it because it was tucked away in a cove of trees. She sucked in air that made a loud whistle as we parked in front of the old, white, two-story plantation house. It was much too big for me alone, but I hoped to fill it one day with my own family.

"Wow," she whispered. "You live here by yourself?"

I sighed deeper than I meant to. "Unfortunately." My eyes

went to her. Callie glanced in my direction and just as quickly averted her gaze, but not before I caught a glimpse of her rose-colored cheeks. I did my best to hide my smirk. "Ya ready?" I asked as I got out and hurried to open her door.

"As I'll ever be," she replied as I helped her down.

How I felt about this woman had me panicking suddenly. Not because of my emotions, but because I was about to introduce her to a kitchen full of other men—*eligible* men. I closed my eyes and sucked in as much air as I could. What was I doing? I guess it couldn't be avoided. I let the air escape. Here goes nothin'.

Chapter 16

Callie

When we arrived inside, the kitchen was buzzing with activity and chatter as everyone had gathered for the meal. I glanced around the room. My eyes grew wide as I realized I was the only female. I wasn't sure how I felt about that.

"Guys!" Colt shouted over everyone. The room became instantly silent as all eyes turned to him, and then they turned to me. Curiosity and confusion stared back at me. Either new residents didn't come around often, or female residents didn't at all. "I wanted to introduce ya to our newest resident at Redemption Ranch. This is Callie St. Claire." There were gasps all around the room. "I know. I know. Just save it." Colt waved his right hand in the air.

What was that about? I looked around the room, searching the faces, hoping to find the answer. It never came.

"Callie, that guy over there is Spencer Wright." Colt pointed to a tall, muscular young guy in a blue shirt and black cowboy hat.

"Callie." He tipped his hat to me.

"Nice to meet you, Spencer."

"That there is Richard Alan." He nodded to the older man at the stove.

Richard wasn't as tall as Spencer, but he was close. He ap-

83

peared to be the oldest in the room. He had dark brown hair and glasses. He nodded.

"Hello, Richard." I waved.

"You already know Jon."

"Nice to see you again, Jon." I nodded in his direction.

"That guy is Austin Collier."

"Hey, Austin," I greeted the stocky, medium-height guy in the corner.

"Next to him is none other than Luke Herring."

I noticed that next to Colt, Luke was the next-best-looking guy in the room, in my opinion anyway, for what it's worth.

"Hi, Luke." I smiled.

"And last, but certainly not least, is Wyatt Glover."

Colt patted Wyatt on the shoulder. Wyatt appeared to be the youngest of the group. He couldn't have been more than eighteen.

"Hi, Wyatt. It's very nice to meet all of you." I glanced down at my clothes and suddenly felt more out of place than I had just a few seconds before. Must be time to shop for some clothes.

"Can we eat now?" Austin asked in a whine. Laughter filled the kitchen. "What? A fat guy's gotta eat," he announced, patting his stomach.

Everyone snickered as they sat. I looked around for a place to sit.

"Callie, you can sit next to me." Luke grinned from ear to ear.

Luke's grin didn't even compare to Colt's in my eyes. I gazed down to where Colt stood at the head of the table, his jaw clenched. I stifled a giggle. He couldn't be jealous, could he? No. I was reading too much into it.

"She'll sit down here," Colt stated through his still-clenched teeth, pulling out the chair next to him.

Was he really telling me where I could or couldn't sit? I looked at the spot in between Luke and Austin, and there was no way this body was going to squish into that small space. I straightened my shoulders, turned up my chin, and strode to the end of the table. "Just because you asked so nicely," I bit back in a sarcastic tone.

"Let's say prayer," Colt stated as he sat, ignoring my snarky comment.

Everyone held hands. Colt took hold of mine, the heat radiating from his hand to mine. Would I ever get used to that? Did he feel it, too?

"Lord, we come to You and ask You to bless this food so we can continue the work You set before us at Redemption Ranch. We thank You for this food and this day. We glorify You. In Jesus' name. Amen."

"Amen," everyone else echoed.

"Let's eat!" Colt announced, picking up the plate of hamburgers and hot dogs.

"Finally!" Austin exclaimed. A round of chuckles filled the air. "What? I'm wastin' away here."

Colt laughed, shook his head, and placed a hamburger and hot dog on his plate before passing it to me. Everyone else did the same with the dishes in front of them. I observed and took a small portion of everything. I wanted to experience all of the delicious food before me but didn't want the table full of men to think I was nothing but a pig at its trough. Looking around the table, though, no one seemed the least bit interested in how much food I put on my plate. My body relaxed.

I enjoyed watching the interaction around the table. It was anything but quiet. Continuous conversation flowed with the occasional bellow of laughter. I wondered if I would ever fit in, being the only woman. Would I ever feel comfortable enough to share stories or joke around? I wanted this ranch to be the place where I belonged. I wanted that *so* much.

"Penny for your thoughts?" Colt leaned over and broke me from my surveillance of the others.

I jumped. "Just enjoying the company."

"Oh?"

"I've been alone so long. I forgot what it's like to have people around a dinner table. Not to mention having to eat a frozen meal. I can definitely get used to this and all these handsome men," I teased him. Colt growled. *Ah, yes. That's the reaction I wanted*, I thought. I did my best to suppress my giggle.

"When we're done eating, do ya want to go see Warrior? It will be time for his nightly meds."

"I'd love to." I beamed at him.

"Great! Eat up!"

Did he mumble something about getting me away from all these men? I giggled softly and ate my food. I was excited to see Warrior since I missed working with him that afternoon. When everyone was finished, I volunteered to clean up since I was new. Much to my surprise, Colt asked to help. "You don't really have to help. I know you have more important things to do," I told him as I let the plates slide from my hands into the sink of soapy water.

"Well, with the two of us, it will go faster, and the more time you'll have with Warrior."

And with you. "Okay." A rush of heat flooded my cheeks. "Thank you."

I hated it when I blushed, but I felt like Colt was always making it happen. Colt and I bantered back and forth as I washed the dishes, and he dried and placed them in their proper cabinets and drawers. It felt unreal to me how easily we fell in tune with each other, especially with mundane domestic chores.

Colt was always so thoughtful. He seemed to put everyone's needs before his own. I wondered who was taking care of him while he was taking care of everyone else. My heart did a little dip. Could it be? Could I be falling in love with him? *Get yourself together, girl. He won't ever feel that way about you,* I heard my aunt say. *Stupid girl.* I berated myself again for what I was feeling for this man. Colt would never return my feelings. It was one thing for him to see me as a friend and another thing entirely for him to see me as more than that. I had tried to keep up the wall I had built around my heart for so many years, but something about the town—the man—had it crashing down from the start. But I needed to steady my emotions, at least when it came to the man.

"Looks like we're all done here. Ready to go?" Colt asked, shaking me out of my inner turmoil. "Ya okay?"

"Yeah. Sorry. Got lost in thought for a minute."

"I see that." He chuckled. "Anything ya want to share?"

My eyes grew large. "No," was all I could manage to let escape. It's all I trusted myself to say in that moment.

"Let's go see your buddy then." Colt smirked.

I breathed a sigh of relief. I found it comforting that Colt didn't pry. He didn't keep pressing to get me to open up. He respected my boundaries. I felt my heart dip again. Yep, I was a goner. We went out to the stable. As soon as I was in the door, Warrior stuck his head out of his stall. I grinned and hurriedly went to him. I needed to get some space between Colt and me. If I didn't, I might have burst into flames. I placed my hands on either side of Warrior's head.

"Hey, boy." I kissed his nose.

Colt coughed gently. "I'll go get his medicine."

"How are you, Warrior?" My hands glided down his side, careful to avoid the wounds that were still healing. I made sure to keep my touch soft and light. Warrior held steady as if he enjoyed my touch. Colt coughed from behind me. I turned and smirked at him.

"Ready for your medicine?" Colt asked. I looked over my shoulder at Warrior as Colt let the feed and pills fall into my hand. Once again, warmth shot straight up my arms. Did he feel it, too?

After burying the pills in the feed, I held out my hands to Warrior. "Here you go. Be a good boy." Warrior lowered his head to my hands, his lips and tongue scooping up the feed without hesitation this time. "That's a good boy." I continued to pet him as he finished chewing. "I'll see you tomorrow. I promise I won't sleep the day away."

"Let's get ya back to your cabin. I'm sure ya'd like to relax a little before bed," Colt suggested.

My heart sank. Since I had accidentally slept all afternoon, I wasn't really tired, but I agreed anyway. "Sure. Okay."

Rejection penetrated my heart, making me question whether or not Colt wanted to spend time with me. Oh well, I could use a little time to relax before I jumped into helping on the ranch. I had never been a ranch hand and didn't know what it entailed, so I wanted to be rested and ready to go for the next day. Maybe I could sit on the porch in the rocking chair and read for a little while.

Colt pulled up to the cabin, and I wished it was further away. I wanted a few more minutes with him. "Well, here we are," he announced.

"Okay. See you tomorrow. What time should I be at the stable?"

"We usually have breakfast at the house from five to six. If ya don't want breakfast, ya can just be at the stable at six."

I gasped. "In the morning? What on God's green Earth could cause anyone to get up before the sun rises?"

Colt chuckled. "There's a lot of work to be done on a ranch. You'll understand better tomorrow. Oh, and make sure ya close your door tight this time. Ya don't want to be woke up by raccoons pillaging your cabin." He chuckled again.

"Um. Okay. Thanks for the ride . . . and the advice." I leaned over the center console and kissed Colt's cheek before jumping down from the truck and hurrying inside. What was I thinking? Obviously, I wasn't.

My lips tingled long after Colt's truck pulled away. What I felt for him couldn't be love, could it? After only a week? I kept asking myself these questions because it just seemed so crazy to me. He wasn't even my boyfriend.

I tried to rationalize it every way I possibly could, but it was no use. I knew there would never be another man to reside in my heart . . . just him. I grabbed my book and a lantern I found in one of the closets and went out onto the porch. It was a beautiful evening. The rocking chair looked worn. Would it hold me? Would I fall through the seat? I slowly lowered myself into the chair, adding a little more of my weight as I sat. The chair creaked. I closed my eyes tight and held my breath, waiting for my backside to hit the ground. When the chair held, I opened my eyes and exhaled. Phew!

I sat outside for a while. It was so peaceful. I couldn't believe how dark it became out here without the lights of a city. The crickets were chirping, and the lightning bugs were lighting up the night sky in every direction. I shot my eyes upward and gasped at the expanse of stars. It was a clear night, so there were stars as far as I could see. I yawned suddenly. How could

I be tired after such a long nap? I didn't fight it. I picked up the lantern and my book and headed inside. I made sure the door was securely closed.

"Happy now, Colt?" I muttered and stuck out my tongue.

I changed into my pajamas and climbed into bed. Exhaustion wrapped around me, snuffing out every last ounce of wakefulness until I succumbed, my eyes refusing to stay open, my consciousness drifting into dreamland.

Chapter 17

Callie

I slowly opened my eyes. I rubbed them before opening them completely to the start of a new day. It was barely light outside. I was giddy about working with Warrior. If I admitted it, I was just as excited, if not more so, to work with Colt. I felt my lips form a smile that spread across all of my face. I was a mess. I covered my face with my hands, shook my head, and giggled. What was wrong with me? I jumped out of bed, grabbed my clothes, and stepped into the shower.

When I felt presentable enough, my hair in a bun and T-shirt and jeans on, I strode out the door. The stable was down the road a ways, but I chose to walk and enjoy the scenery. The trees danced in the breeze, causing their scent to drift down to me. My lips turned upward, as did my face, to allow the breeze to caress my face. Wildflowers lined the dirt road every few feet. I plucked one that was yellow around the edges but turned into a fiery orange near the center. The center was a dark brown circle. I had no idea what kind of flower it was, but it was beautiful.

When I stepped into the stable, Colt was already there, pulling apart a hay bale. "Hey there," I greeted.

He glanced in my direction. "Stealing already, huh?" He nodded toward the flower in my hand and chuckled.

I felt the warmth come to my cheeks. I smiled shyly and gazed at the ground. "Yeah. Sorry."

"No need to be sorry." He chuckled once more. "I was just kiddin'."

"Oh." I tried to giggle, but only air escaped. "So, what can I do?"

"Well." He stepped over to a cabinet, pulled out a pair of work gloves, and tossed them to me. "Put those on, and ya can help me put hay in the stalls. Better say hi to Warrior first. He's been waitin' on ya." He nodded toward Warrior's stall.

"Okay." I pulled my bottom lip between my teeth before going over to Warrior. He poked his head out. "Hey there, handsome." I ran my hand up Warrior's nose. "How are you, boy?"

"Here's his medicine," Colt spoke from behind me.

I turned to find Colt's arm extended to me with feed and pills in his hand. I cupped my hands under his. He poured the contents into them. I was disappointed when his hand didn't touch mine. I wanted to feel the heat that always accompanied the contact. A shiver crawled down my spine. What was going on with me? I did the best I could to hide my disappointment.

"Here, Warrior. Time for some food." My voice stayed calm and steady, even though my insides shook. Warrior didn't hesitate to take the food. I was so proud that he trusted me. I ran my fingers through his white mane at the top of his head. "Good boy!" I turned back to find Colt watching intently. I felt my lips turn upward into a grin as the heat popped into my cheeks. "Okay. What's next?"

"Well, you can help me finish making sure each stall has hay in it, and then we can take Warrior for a walk if ya'd like."

"I'd love to." I pulled the heavy work gloves onto my hands. "I'm ready." I clapped my hands together. "What do I do?"

"Just take some hay in your hands from the bale and plop it in each of the stalls. Like this." He pulled some hay free and tossed it in the nearest stall.

"Okay. That looks easy enough." I tugged at the bale, but nothing budged. I tugged again and went flying backward, hay and my arms flailing in every direction. I waited for my body to thud against the ground, but instead, arms were around me.

"I got ya," Colt whispered into my ear.

"Thank you." I did my best to regain my composure and my pride.

"Ya okay?" He asked, setting me upright.

"Yeah. Just a little embarrassed is all." I wiped the hay off my pants and shirt.

"Oh, don't be. It happens more often than ya might think." Colt plucked a piece of hay from my hair.

"Maybe we should try something else." I giggled nervously.

"How about *I* will pull the hay free, and you can put it in the stalls? Then, we can take Warrior for a walk."

"That sounds like a good idea. Don't need me claiming Workman's Comp on the first day." I laughed heartily, which caused Colt to laugh, too.

When the stalls all had hay, Colt grabbed a halter and a lead rope. He stood next to me and handed me the halter.

"Tell me what I need to do."

"I'll put the lead rope on, and you can put the halter on." He nodded toward the device he had given me.

"Okay." I glanced up at him as I bit my bottom lip.

"I'll walk ya through it. Don't worry." He looped the lead rope around Warrior's neck. "Okay. Ya wanna be on his left side near his shoulder. Hold the buckle in ya left hand and the strap in ya right."

"Like this?" I asked, furrowing my brows.

"Exactly. Now, reach under his neck with your right hand and guide his nose into the noseband. That's it. Ya got it. Bring the strap over the top of his head just behind his ears. That's right. Now, attach it to the buckle on his left cheek."

"I did it!" I beamed and kissed Warrior's cheek.

"Now, we lead him out of the stall." He passed me the lead rope.

I took the rope and guided Warrior out. At first, he stood his ground.

"Come on, buddy. Let's go get some fresh air." I pleaded with him. I pulled lightly on the rope, and we moved forward. We led him around the area near the stable. "This land is so beautiful."

"Thank you. I *do* love it here."

"I can see why. So, what made you decide to start Redemption Ranch? I'm assuming it wasn't always this kind of ranch."

"No, it wasn't." Colt leaned down to pluck a tall blade of grass. He tore little pieces off as he told me the story of the ranch. "When I re-dedicated my life to Christ, I realized the magnitude of His mercy, forgiveness, and grace. I wanted others to get a chance to know and experience it also. I wanted to help people and animals. Every man that lives and works here has a story. I don't know if it's *all* God has for me, but if it is, I will always do it with gratitude."

"I love that."

"You do?" He glanced at me with raised brows.

"Yes. I re-dedicated my life to Christ last year. I'm not sure of my purpose yet, but I know God led me here for some reason. I wish He would show me, or at least give me patience."

We walked a little longer before making our way back to the stable.

"Well, it looks like we missed lunch," Colt informed me as he looked at his watch.

"That's okay. I'm not that hungry."

"Do ya want to continue to work, and then I'll take ya out for supper?"

"That sounds nice." My cheeks warmed. "You know, if I wasn't mistaken, I'd think you like making me blush."

He didn't say a word. He just shrugged and grinned sheepishly. We settled Warrior in his stall before mucking out the others. I learned quickly that was not my favorite chore in the slightest. We completed the rest of the chores Colt said we needed to do.

"Whew!" I wiped the sweat from my forehead with my arm.

I saw Colt's shoulders move up and down in a chuckle out of the corner of my eye. "Well, let's go get cleaned up, and we'll get some supper together," he suggested.

"You don't want to eat with everyone else?"

"Is that okay with ya?"

"It's perfectly fine. I just wondered."

"Do ya want a ride to the cabin?"

"Do you mind?" I glanced up at him.

"Not at all. Come on." He motioned for me to follow him. He opened the passenger door for me before jogging around to the other side.

When he pulled up to my cabin, he shut off the engine. "So, I'll pick ya up in an hour?" he asked.

"Forty-five minutes should do it unless *you* need longer." I giggled.

"Forty-five minutes it is."

"Okay. See you soon." I grinned at him. I jumped down from my perch in his truck and hurried inside. I let out a huge breath as soon as the door shut. Wow! That was tough work. I hoped it would get easier as time went on.

I picked out my outfit of jeans, boots, and a green blouse. After my shower, I braided my hair, got dressed, and dabbed on some makeup. I added a little bit of light-green eye shadow to my eyes before swiping the mascara on my lashes. As soon as I shut off the bathroom light, a knock sounded on my door. My heart did a somersault. I grabbed my small, crossbody purse and threw it over my shoulder and head before opening the door.

The sight of Colt had my feet cemented to the floor. My breath caught in my throat. He was wearing black jeans, black boots, and a black cowboy hat with a sapphire-blue shirt that made his steel-blue eyes practically glow.

"Wow!"

"What?" He moved his hands down the front of his shirt. "Is something wrong? Do I look bad?"

"Not. At. All." I scanned him from his toes to his head before my eyes met his.

"Thanks." He lifted his hat off his head and ran his hand through his hair. His eyes gave me a once over. "Callie." He let out a breath. "You look amazing."

"Thanks." I bit my bottom lip.

"Well, are ya ready to go?" He extended his arm toward his truck.

"I am." I smiled.

After we arrived at the restaurant just off the bay, Colt helped me out of the truck, placed his hand at the small of my back, and guided me inside. As we ate, we talked about the day.

"Well, I survived. I don't think I'm going to have trouble falling asleep tonight. That's for sure." I giggled. "But I enjoyed it . . . well, except the manure. Definitely not my favorite."

Colt laughed. "Yeah, not mine either, but someone's gotta do it."

"True. Thank you for showing me the ropes." I gazed in his direction.

"You're welcome. I had a good time." He held my stare.

I moved my eyes to my hands folded in my lap. We finished our meal, and Colt paid the check. "Would ya like to go for a walk?" he asked.

I was conflicted because I was exhausted, but I didn't want my time with him to end. I opened my mouth to decline. "I'd like that." My words betrayed me.

"After you then." He extended his arm and hand.

We walked out onto the pier. The sun was disappearing behind the trees. The sky was painted in yellow, red, and orange fading into black. The pier was quiet as we were the only ones there. If it had been a date, it would've been the epitome of romantic. *Don't get any ideas, stupid girl. Get your head out of the clouds*, my aunt's voice told me. I leaned against the rail, trying to erase her voice from my mind.

"Such a beautiful night." Colt broke the silence.

"It truly is."

The moon was rising in the sky, casting a majestic reflection on the water. It definitely was a beautiful night. I didn't need words from the man standing next to me. His presence alone filled me with so much happiness. I could have burst. "I should probably get you home," he said softly in my ear.

"Okay." I did my best to plaster a grin on my face. The air from Colt's words tickling my ear long after they disappeared. I wasn't ready, but I knew the day had to end eventually.

We arrived back at the cabin, and Colt walked me to the door. "Thank you for dinner, Colt. I had a nice time."

"Me, too."

I hugged him, kissed his cheek, and went into the cabin.

"Make sure ya close that door tight," he called out just before the door closed completely.

As the door latched, I giggled.

Chapter 18

Colt

It was finally the Fourth of July. I couldn't wait to share the festival with Callie. She said she hadn't experienced festivals before, so I wanted to make sure she got a taste of them all in Edenton. Next to the Harvest Festival, The Fourth of July Festival was my favorite. I parked in front of Callie's cabin and jumped out, giddy to see her. I saw her every day, but the excitement never seemed to fade away.

"Are ya ready to go?" I asked when she opened the door. When I glanced at her, I gasped. She looked stunning with her hair piled up on top of her head in a messy bun and wearing a coral-colored dress with pale yellow flowers on it. It went down to just about her knees. She paired it with a pair of cowgirl boots. "Wow." I suddenly felt parched.

"You like it?"

"I do."

"Coral is my favorite color." She grinned at me.

"It looks amazing on ya."

"Thank you." I caught a glimpse of her blush before she gazed down at the ground.

"Ready?"

"Yes. I'm so excited." She beamed.

"You're going to love this. It's one of my favorites." I really was more excited to spend the entire day with her. I didn't care where it was. I parked the truck in the first space I could find in town. "Looks like we are gonna have to hoof it a bit. That okay? I can always drop ya off closer and find a place to park."

"Walking is fine." The way her lips turned up into a smile melted me.

As we made our way to the county courthouse, we took time to chat with people. Anyone with whom Callie wasn't familiar, I made sure to introduce her. We stopped in at Courageous Café and Bakery to see Marci and Caitlyn. They agreed to meet up with us that evening for the fireworks.

When we got to the crowd surrounding the front of the courthouse, I turned to Callie. "This is awesome. The festival kicks off with an annual reading of the Declaration of Independence. The guy who reads it is dressed in 1776 attire." I glanced over at Callie. She wore a huge grin. I shrugged. "What?"

"Nothing." She giggled. "You're just adorable when you're excited."

"I'm sorry." I ran my fingers through my hair. "I love history."

"I do, too." She beamed.

After the reading, we headed down to the waterfront. There were vendors set up all over the park just opposite the water.

"Oh. There's Olivia. Can we go say hi?"

"We can do anything ya like today, Callie." I grinned at her.

She grabbed my hand and pulled me over to Olivia's booth. "Hey, Olivia!" Callie called out before reaching out to give Olivia a hug.

"Hey, Cal. How are ya?" Olivia had started calling Callie

that a few weeks ago. I wasn't sure why. "Hey, Colt."

"Hi, Olivia. What do you have this go-round?"

"Just a few pieces. Have a look." She motioned to the table.

"Oh. Olivia. They're amazing! Oh. I love this one." Callie pointed to a landscape of a pond surrounded by trees and flowers of various colors.

I took notice that the canvas had colors of orange, coral, and yellow. The colors Callie seemed to be partial to. I motioned for Olivia to step away and whispered, "Can ya put that aside for her? I'll pay ya for it. Would make a great birthday present, don't ya think?"

Olivia grinned. "As soon as you leave, I'll do that."

"Thanks." I smiled and touched her shoulder. "You're a gem."

"I know." She beamed.

"Olivia, these are all so beautiful. I'll see you later?" Callie asked.

"Yep. Let's meet up at the fireworks?"

"Absolutely." Callie hugged Olivia one last time before we moved on to other things.

There was someone riding the mechanical bull. Callie watched with wide eyes, and her shoulders shook with laughter. I loved watching her experience the festival. That may have been my favorite part. The watermelon-eating contest was in full swing by the time we arrived. We joined the gathering crowd. Everyone was chanting and cheering on their favorite contestant.

"Is that Dylan?" Callie asked. Dylan was Marci and Chuck's son.

"Where?" I tried to see over everyone's heads from the back of the crowd. "Yeah, I think it is. GO, DYLAN!" I cheered.

"And the winner is . . ." The announcer paused a few minutes after the contest ended. "Dylan Logan."

"WOOT WOOT! WAY TO GO, DYLAN!" Callie called out, cupping her hands around her mouth. It made me chuckle to watch her get so excited for Dylan. "Oh, my goodness. That was awesome! I can't believe Dylan ate that much watermelon." Her head fell back with laughter.

Leaning to her ear, I asked, "Are ya having a good time?"

"I'm having the best time. Thank you for bringing me here. I can see why you like this festival so much." As we passed the buckets of seeds that had been removed from the watermelon, she asked, "What do they do with all those seeds?"

"Seed-spitting contest, of course," I stated matter-of-factly.

"Of course." She rolled her eyes.

"Do ya wanna watch?"

"Um . . . no."

"Are ya hungry? They usually have amazing hot dogs."

"A man after my own heart," she stated, placing her hand on her stomach.

If she only knew. I'd give just about anything to be the man of her heart. But I'd have to settle for being friends because being friends was better than not having her in my life at all. We trekked over to where the food vendors were located. "Two hot dogs, please," I ordered. "The toppings are over there." I motioned to a table by the seating area.

I handed Callie one of the hot dogs and escorted her to the topping table. I glanced at her as she added ketchup and relish to hers. Simple woman—I liked it. I put the same on mine. We took seats at a nearby table.

"Thank you again, Colt. This has been such a wonderful afternoon." She laid her hand on mine, and the warmth radiated on my hand. Would that ever stop happening?

"No problem. I've had a great afternoon also. Seems this year's festival has been the best one yet." I grinned at her, and the grin grew when the blush crept up her cheeks. I glanced over at a vendor table and said, "I'll be right back." I stood and left her there.

I paid the vendor and selected the perfect one. When I returned to the table, I extended my hand. "For you."

Callie gasped. "Oh, Colt. It's beautiful. How did you know white roses are my favorite?"

"Lucky guess?" I grinned sheepishly. "I'm glad you like it." She beamed up at me. She was truly a beautiful woman. I hoped one day she would be mine. If it was in God's will, I knew it would happen. "Ya want to check out some other vendors before the fireworks? I think I saw some jewelry vendors over there." I pointed to my left, which took us a little up Broad Street.

"I'd love to." She smiled as she stood from the table.

I took the hot dog wrappers from her hand and threw them in the trash can. "Shall we then?" I extended my hand to motion Callie forward.

"We shall." She grinned.

We stopped at a jewelry table closest to where we had been eating.

"Oh. They have Claddagh rings." Callie's voice changed to a soft affection.

"You like those?" I asked with a surprised tone.

"Yes! I've always wanted one. When I dream of the perfect wedding ring, this is it." She beamed.

Noted. We continued to explore the festival. "Do ya want to go swimming during the fireworks? There's a small beach off the bay. We can watch the fireworks from there. We can invite the Logans and Olivia."

"Uh . . . sure." She glanced down at the ground.

"Ya don't seem so sure. We don't have to if ya aren't comfortable."

"No. I want to." She half-grinned.

"Let's go back to the ranch and get swimming stuff."

"Okay."

"By the time we get back, it should be just about time for the fireworks display."

"Sounds good."

Something had changed. Callie seemed to go back to being reserved. Maybe she felt self-conscious about being in a swimsuit. I couldn't wait to see her in her suit. *Lord, give me strength.*

On our way out to the ranch, I called the Logans and Olivia. They all agreed to meet us at the beach. I waited outside as Callie changed into her suit. She had a coverup on and flip-flops when she returned to the truck. She had tied her hair back in a ponytail.

"Ready," she told me, jumping back into the passenger side.

"Let's go to my house, and I'll change. Then, we'll head out."

"Sounds good."

It was Callie's turn to wait in the truck. I went inside and flew up the stairs. I changed into my trunks and grabbed two towels out of the linen closet. A few minutes later, we were on our way. We were the first ones on the beach.

"Pick a spot, Callie. Any spot."

"How about over here?" She strode over to a little spot on the corner of the beach.

"Looks perfect." Why did she want to be away from where everyone else would be? I shrugged and laid the towels on the sand. Everyone else arrived and immediately splashed into the water. "Do ya want to go in?" I asked her.

"Sure."

We stood and went to the edge of the water. We slowly waded through it. Callie stopped when the water got to her waist. I had already gone under the water and come back up for air. "Come on in, Callie. It feels great." The water was the perfect temperature. It wasn't too cold but enough to cool off from the warmer temperature of the day.

"I'm okay right here."

"Come on," Dylan and Caitlyn begged in unison.

"I'm really okay right here. Really."

I playfully splashed her, then moved closer to grab her hand.

"Colt, please. I'm really okay *right* here." She moved her hand out of reach.

"Callie, what's wrong?" I stood next to her.

"I just don't want to go any deeper in the water, okay?" Her voice became harsher as she turned and trudged back to the beach. "Olivia!" She hollered, striding over to where Olivia was on the beach. "Can you take me home?"

I didn't hear the rest of the conversation, but Callie grabbed the towel, wrapped it around her lower body, and followed Olivia off the beach. Would I ever get it right with her? I smacked the water on the surface, and the splash covered me. I let out a frustrated growl.

With confusion swimming around in my head long after I left the water and the beach, I drove home. The events played on repeat in my mind. Was Callie afraid of water? Did she not know how to swim? All I knew was I needed to get out of these wet clothes and then find Callie to apologize for pushing her to do something she obviously didn't want to. I didn't want to be like others in her life. I wanted to be different.

I sped down the dirt driveway, kicking up dust as I skidded to a stop at my house. As soon as I was inside, I stripped off my trunks, hopping on one foot as one leg hole clung to my ankle. The trunks finally released my foot, and I grabbed a pair of jeans and a T-shirt. I closed the front door as I looked down. Dang it! No shoes. Oh well. My heart was in overdrive and needed to find out if Callie was okay. To make things right.

As I inched to a stop, turning off the headlights just before reaching Callie's cabin, I noticed her silhouette in the window. I crept closer. It appeared as if she was crying, her body shaking, her head in her hands. What the heck did I do wrong?

I stepped onto the wooden porch, raised my hand to knock, and sucked in a breath. Something poked the bottom of my foot. I raised my right foot to my left knee to see a quarter-inch sliver protruding from the ball of my foot. I tugged on the end, but the other half stayed embedded. Ugh! If I didn't get it out, it would get infected.

Then, it hit me. It was a lightbulb moment if I ever had one. Whatever had happened to Callie was still deeply embedded in her soul, not yet ready to be expelled. And I couldn't remove it for her. The revelation brought a pang to my heart. It had to be her and God.

I hobbled to the truck, careful not to put pressure that would cause the intruder to dig deeper into my foot. I'd screwed up enough in my life. I didn't want to screw this up any worse with Callie.

Glancing back at the woman in the window, the one I so desperately wanted to hug and console, I slid into my truck and slowly drove home. Maybe one day, she would tell me what I did wrong. Then again, maybe she wouldn't.

Chapter 19

Callie

It was a gorgeous late July morning. Colt and I went about our days since the Fourth of July like the night at the beach didn't happen. Maybe one day, I would tell him why I couldn't go in the water. It was a Sunday, and we had arrived at the church. It was quaint. Small. Perfect. Not a large church, which is what I loved. I hated large groups. With its whitewashed exterior and high steeple topped with a cross, the church was the epitome of a country church. The natural brown doors to the entrance contrasted well. The stained-glassed windows cascaded a prism of colors into the church when the sun shone through them. The mahogany pews were stiff and, at least, helped keep postures straight. Pastor Steve greeted us at the door. I had been attending the church since the end of June, so only a couple of weeks.

"Good morning, Colt." He shook Colt's hand. "Good morning, Callie." He nodded. "So great to have you both here this morning."

"Mornin'," Colt responded as he placed his hand on the small of my back.

"Morning, Pastor." I nodded and smiled.

Colt ushered me inside. Just inside the door was the Logan family.

"Mornin', Logan family." Colt stretched his hand to shake Chuck's hand.

"Morning, Marci, Caitlyn." I grinned at them before giving each of them a hug.

As we made our way down the aisle, I waved at Edna Perry, a widowed woman from whom Olivia rented an apartment that was connected to her house. Edna waved before returning to her conversation. I stopped to hug Marie and Carl. Carl had been doing well since his heart attack. He and Marie could be seen trekking up and down Broad Street holding hands. I hoped to have that someday. Colt motioned me to the pew in front of Marie and Carl.

"Can I sit with you, Callie?" Caitlyn appeared at the end of the pew.

"Of course." I beamed up at her.

I scooted closer to Colt to make room. Pastor Steve took his place at the pulpit. He led the congregation in prayer before beginning his sermon.

"Today, we're going to delve into the crucifixion and everything Christ experienced for us so we don't have to suffer for our sins." He bent down, and when he rose again, he had something in his hand. "Now, before Christ got to the cross, he was beaten with a whip with many leather strands and pieces of metal or bone that stuck out on the ends. They beat him." He cracked the whip against a table.

The sound the whip made had my back board straight. My grip was so tight on the pew that my knuckles were white, and nausea bubbled up in my stomach. I knew that sound better than any other sound in the world. In an attempt to tamper down the vomit swirling around in my stomach, I closed my eyes. I was transported back to the time with my aunt. The stench of stale cigarettes and cat urine invaded my nostrils. I could hear the faint sound of my aunt's voice berating me. She found any excuse to crack that whip on my back. Even no excuse at all.

When the whip hit the table again, the nausea moved to my throat. I began to see white spots, and I almost jumped out of the pew.

"Callie, are ya okay?" I barely heard Colt ask through the ringing in my ears.

I made a quick exit to the ladies' room and lost what I had eaten in two days, or so it felt. When I could expel no more, and the nausea finally dissipated, I cupped my hands under the sink faucet and rinsed the remnants from my mouth. I ripped off a paper towel to dry my hand, mouth, and forehead. The humidity in the bathroom was enough to strangle the air from my lungs. I needed air desperately. I snuck out of the bathroom and held my breath, praying I wouldn't hear that sound again. I tiptoed outside as quickly as I could. I inhaled deeply, trying to fill my lungs with clean air and to get the smell of my aunt's home out of my nose.

"Callie?" Colt asked quietly. He placed his hand on my back, and I flinched. It was like I had just received a backlashing. The pressure of his touch stung, and it took all my strength not to jerk away. I willed back the tears that threatened. "What happened? What's wrong?"

I turned and faced him. "I'm sorry. I had to get out of there. That sound . . ." My lip quivered.

"What's wrong?" he inquired again, concern growing in his voice.

I sucked in as much air as I could and exhaled. It was time to tell him. *Lord, help me find the words.* I told him what no other soul knew aside from my aunt and Warrior.

"My aunt," I started, "used to use a whip on me. She used

to strike my back with it for any reason and no reason. I'm not sure why. After a while, I stopped feeling anything. I just escaped into myself. The sound of that whip just took me back there." The tears began to fall.

"Oh, Callie." Colt wrapped his arm around my shoulders. "So that's why ya didn't want to take your coverup off at the beach." I nodded, not trusting my voice in that moment. "I'm so sorry, Callie. If I had known . . ."

"You didn't. It's okay."

"That's why you and Warrior have such a strong bond, isn't it? That's what ya meant when you said you wish you didn't know such cruelty." I nodded again. I couldn't find my voice because my heart was in my throat. "Let's get ya out of here, okay? Come on, sweetie." He took my hand and guided me to his truck.

Colt drove me home in silence. I didn't have the energy to speak. I wasn't sure I could. I didn't even know where he drove me at first. When we arrived at our destination, Colt led me inside. "Here, sit here. I'll have someone go to your cabin to get ya something to change into. You're going to stay here tonight. I don't want ya to be alone."

I nodded in response. I heard Colt in the other room tell one of the guys to go to my cabin and bring back some clothes. The next thing I heard was Colt whispering to me to wake up. I sat up on the couch as he handed me some clothes.

"Thank you," I whispered before going into the bathroom to change.

When I came back out, Colt came from the kitchen with a glass of water. "Here. I thought ya might need a drink."

"Thank you." My lip trembled. I couldn't stop the tears from falling. Why was he being so nice to me? Why did he still act like he cared? I was a fat freak. Why didn't he just drop me off at my cabin and tell me it was time for me to leave? Before I could even formulate some sort of answer, Colt's arms were around me.

"It's going to be okay, Callie. I'm not going to let anyone hurt ya ever again."

I laid my head on his leg as he ran his hand up and down my arm. I let the darkness overtake me. I just wanted the day to be over.

* * *

Colt

I watched as Callie slept. Never had I ever seen red faster than when she told me what her aunt had done to her. Tears stung my eyes. I wanted to go to Indiana and knock some sense into her aunt. I knew vengeance wasn't something God liked, so I shook the thought from my mind. It probably wouldn't have worked anyway. It all explained so much about Callie and her lack of trust. I wanted to protect her from anything bad that could happen to her. I played with her hair. My heart swelled as I gazed down at her sleeping form. What was I going to do with my feelings for her? I just had to learn to control them before they controlled me. There was no way she would ever feel the same about me. I would have to take things as they came as far as she was concerned. I just hoped my heart could survive.

Chapter 20

Callie

Over the next few weeks, neither Colt nor I discussed that day at church. No one in town really asked about my quick departure from the church that morning either. I was relieved. I guess the rumor mill took care of itself on that matter.

I continued to work with Colt and Warrior. Warrior was almost back to 100 percent. Both had become my very best friends. Neither Colt nor I made a move to make our relationship anything other than friends. I accepted it because I knew he would never return my feelings, and I would rather have him as a friend than nothing at all. We continued to go almost everywhere together. I continued to go to church. I prayed for God to give me the strength to continue going after that Sunday, and He did.

I arose to a beautiful end-of-August morning. The temperature was a perfect 86 degrees, and everything was still so green. The birds were chirping in the trees. I was excited as always to spend time with Warrior and made sure to get to the stable while all the guys were still at breakfast. I loved coming to the stable—the mixture of horses, hay, leather, and of course, the ever-dreaded manure. Mucking the stalls was still not my favorite. Yuck!

Warrior, though, was a special kind of horse. It was like

our spirits were connected by the tragedies that had happened to us. He understood me in a way no human had, and I understood the cruelty he had endured just as I had. I didn't have to imagine what he had been through because I had lived it, and by the grace of God, survived it. I knew I would continue to show him what love looked like every day for the rest of his life.

"Hey, Warrior. You want to go for a walk?" I asked, grabbing a lead and halter.

While Warrior had come a long way from where he had been, no one was able to ride him yet, but I walked him as much as I could. His wounds were completely healed but had left many scars all over his body. As we sauntered away from the stable, I talked to Warrior as if he was an old friend. I found our time together very therapeutic. I told Warrior things I couldn't tell humans, like what my heart was telling me about Colt. He was also the first I told about the things my aunt had done to me. Warrior didn't judge me or put me down or look at me with pity in his eyes. He just listened.

"My birthday is coming up next week. It hasn't been a good day in a long time. Maybe I could spend the day with you to make it more bearable. It has just been so hard to celebrate on the day my parents were taken from me, ya know?"

Warrior snorted as if he understood. It made me grin. We continued our hike, and I continued to confide in him. As we progressed further through the prairie-type grass, we encountered a narrow creek. I slipped off my shoes and socks and rolled up my pant legs. I searched out a stone to step onto, trying not to slip. I held my breath with each step, waiting to splash into the water. The freezing water pricked my feet.

As I stepped out onto the grass on the other side of the water, an intense pain engulfed my ankle. I cried out as I peered down to see two puncture wounds. The grass was moving, and I tried to catch a glimpse of what bit me. Was that brown thing what bit me, or was it just grass and mud? I didn't know for sure. Within seconds, my ankle was on fire. I tried to continue to put pressure on it, but it was too excruciating. I limped over to the big tree, wincing with every step, my ankle already turning red and swelling. I backed up against the tree, using it for leverage as I lowered myself to the ground.

"Warrior, I need you to go get help." I cried loudly because Warrior just stood there as if he didn't want to leave me. "What am I going to do? There's no way I will make it back to the stable. Warrior! Go, boy! Go get Colt!"

At my command, Warrior finally bolted in the direction of the stable. Dizziness swirled in my head as nausea pummeled my stomach. *Please don't puke.* To take myself away from the pain, I did what I always did when my aunt grabbed her whip: I closed my eyes and recalled the last time I was with my parents. The euphoria began to take over, and Colt flashed through my mind.

Chapter 21

Colt

I was surprised when Callie didn't show up for breakfast. Throughout the meal, I kept glancing at the door. As breakfast drew to a close and everyone dispersed to work on their chores for the day, I left the dirty dishes in the sink, which I had never done, and hurried to the stable, hoping to find Callie there with Warrior. Finding his stall empty and neither of them to be seen, I figured she must have taken him for a stroll, so I got to work mucking out the stalls. A bad feeling settled in the pit of my stomach. I was just being overprotective. That had to be it.

In the middle of mucking out Warrior's stall, my attention turned toward the door as the distinct pounding of hoof beats grew closer—not a walking horse, but one racing toward the stable. Was Callie riding Warrior? This I had to see. I ran outside, both scared and excited to see if Callie had finally tamed Warrior.

Fear punched me in the gut. Warrior was alone. Where was Callie? The horse paced in circles, whinnying and stomping his hooves. I had to move slow—had to keep Warrior calm. It was clear he still didn't trust me completely. I paused, and even though my pulse revved at dangerous levels, I spoke in a low, tranquil tone. "Warrior, where's Callie?"

Warrior took a few steps toward me but stopped a few feet

short of standing right in front of me as if he was leery of getting any closer. When I searched Warrior's eyes, I swore I saw worry and fear. Warrior reared up and let out a high-pitched squeal. He turned in the direction from which he came. I didn't have time to saddle up Beauty. Without thinking, I jumped on Warrior's back, and we took off in a sprint. I prayed Warrior would take me to Callie and that she was okay. As Warrior raced through the tall grass, the sound was like a machete wiping out the stalks in one fell swoop. Luckily, on this part of the ranch, there were no thickets, so I didn't have to worry about being bombarded by limbs and brush beating me in the face.

As we approached the creek, Callie came into view. She was propped up against my favorite tree and looked as if she was sleeping. Before Warrior even came to a stop, I jumped down and rushed to her.

"Sweetheart, wake up." I ran the backs of my fingers down her cheek. "Come on, baby, ya need to wake up." I tried to remain calm, but everything inside of me wanted to spiral out of control. When she didn't stir, I leaned in close and whispered, "Callie, please wake up." I scanned her body for wounds of any kind. Her skin was pale, and her breathing was shallow. When I glanced toward her feet, I saw her bulging, red ankle. I immediately noticed the puncture wounds.

I shook her to see if she would respond. "Callie." I leaned in and kissed her lips. It worked in the Disney movies, didn't it? I had tried everything else.

Callie began to whimper. "Colt?" she asked, opening her eyes.

I couldn't believe it worked! "Yes, sweetheart. It's me. What happened?"

"I think a snake bit me. I didn't know what else to do but

send Warrior."

"Did you see what it looked like?" I cradled her in my arms.

"It was brown, I think, with hourglass shapes all over its body?"

"Sounds like a Copperhead. They're common 'round here."

Copperheads weren't usually deadly. I didn't know if she was having an allergic reaction to the venom or if it was something else. Allergic reactions weren't common, but they'd been known to happen.

"I guess *everyone* loves me in Edenton." She tried to giggle.

"At least ya still have your sense of humor." I chuckled a little and shook my head. "We need to get ya out of here and get some medical attention. Do ya think ya can stand up and walk over to Warrior?" As soon as I said his name, Warrior was at my side.

"I'm okay, buddy. Thank you for bringing help." Callie reassured Warrior as I helped her to her feet. Warrior attempted to nuzzle her neck as if he wanted to make sure for himself that she was okay. As Callie wrapped her arm around me for support, she softly said, "Thank you for coming to rescue me, Colt." Her breath on my cheek had goosebumps forming on my arms. I helped her hobble a few steps to Warrior's side.

"This is going to be rough and painful, but you can do it." I leaned down and linked my hands together for Callie to put her foot in so I could help hoist her up. "Okay. Grab hold of Warrior's mane at the base of his neck. Then, grab hold just under your hand holding the mane, and fling your leg over his back. I'm going to lift ya up."

"Okay," Callie said with a slight crackle in her voice as she grabbed Warrior's mane.

117

"Ya got this, Callie. You can do this. On the count of three . . . one . . . two . . . three." I boosted her up and saw she was able to get her leg over Warrior's back. "Ya good?"

"Yeah. I think so."

"Okay. I'm going to jump on behind you."

I grabbed Warrior's mane before lifting myself onto his back. Once we were both settled, I squeezed my thighs against Warrior's sides to get him in motion. We went as fast as Callie could handle. She leaned into my chest. I felt completely helpless. *Hold yourself together, Colt. She needs you. Don't let her down.*

"Stay with me, Callie. We're going to get help," I whispered in her ear.

In record time, we were back at the stable. As we approached, Jon came out.

"Jon, can ya help me get her down and then go get my truck? She was bit by a Copperhead, and I'm not sure what's going on. She passed out on the ride here."

Jon and I struggled to get her down, but we finally succeeded. We laid her on the ground, and I cradled her in my arms while waiting for Jon to arrive with the truck. He parked next to us and helped me get her in the back seat.

"Okay, Jon. We're in. Drive as fast as you can."

It didn't take long to get to the hospital. As soon as Jon stopped at the entrance to the emergency room, I jumped out and ran inside. "Help! I need help out here!" Nurses and Doctor Mitchell came running.

"What's going on?" Doctor Mitchell asked.

"She was bit by a snake. From what she described when I found her, it was a Copperhead. She passed out on the way back to the stable, and she hasn't woken up since. Please, help her," I begged.

They got her out of the truck and onto a gurney. Doc Mitchell stopped me when they began to enter the emergency room bay areas. "I'll come and get you when we've got something for you."

My nerves were on high alert. I couldn't stop pacing. Nausea brewed in my stomach. Not good. What the heck was she thinking? Questions bombarded from every direction. Why did she go off alone? Why didn't she tell me? Didn't she realize how dangerous that was?

I didn't know how long Callie had been out there to determine the speed with which her ankle had swelled. Where was the doctor? What was taking so long? Didn't they know I needed to be in there with her? It seemed like it was a decade before Doc Mitchell came out to find me.

"Colt." He strode over to me. "We've given her some antivenom. I don't believe she passed out due to the venom, but rather because her body went into shock as well as her low blood pressure. She's going to be okay. We just have to give her body time to rest. We're going to keep her here at least until tomorrow for observation. She may be here a few days, but we're going to take it one day at a time."

"Can I see her?" I ran my fingers through my hair and massaged the back of my neck.

"As soon as we get her upstairs and in a room, I'll send a nurse to come get you and take you to her."

"Okay." I stuffed my hands in my pockets. Tears stung my eyes, and my chest tightened. I had never felt so helpless in my entire life. It felt like a lifetime before the nurse came to get me.

"Follow me." The nurse motioned with her hand.

We traveled down the hall to the elevators. We ascended to the second floor. When we arrived at room 212, the nurse opened the door. There was Callie, her eyes still closed. Oh, how I longed to see her beautiful green eyes. I immediately went to the chair that was beside the bed, sat, and took hold of her hand. *God, please don't take her away from me. I haven't had the chance to tell her I love her.*

Tell her now, My Son.

I opened my eyes and glanced around the room. Hearing the voice of God didn't happen to me often, but it never ceased to amaze me. I could feel the floodgates of my heart bursting open. I leaned down so my mouth was close to Callie's ear. I didn't want anyone else but her to hear what I was going to tell her.

"Callie, I know we haven't known each other that long, but I am so in love with you. I want to spend the rest of my life showing you, so I need ya to wake up, baby."

I had no idea why I suddenly called her all those pet names. I always made a conscious effort not to. Maybe it was because I was in crisis mode? Who knew?

Chapter 22

Callie

I stood from the base of the tree. I must have fallen asleep. Warrior was grazing on nearby grass. "Hey, boy. Why'd you let me fall asleep? Guess we should head back. I don't want anyone to worry. I didn't plan on being gone this long."

I led Warrior back to the stable. When we arrived, Colt came out to greet us. "There you are!" he exclaimed, enveloping me in his arms and lifting me off the ground.

I was caught off guard as Colt had never done that before. I liked it. When my feet were back on the ground, I glanced up at him through my lashes. His face wore a serious expression—one I'd never experienced. He leaned in closer. I thought—no, I hoped—he was going to kiss me. My heart did a somersault in my chest.

Colt put his mouth to my ear and whispered, "Callie, I know we haven't known each other that long, but I am so in love with you. I want to spend the rest of my life showing you . . ."

My heart almost pounded out of my chest. I couldn't believe he was confessing his love for me. This can't be real, can it? Is this just a dream?

"I need you to wake up, baby," Colt finished as he began to disappear right before my eyes.

Wake up? What did he mean? I'm standing right here.

"*What do you mean? Where are you going?*" *I began to cry. My whole body shook. I was completely confused and scared. I twirled around in every direction.* "*Colt!*" *I yelled as loud as I could, but he was no longer there.*

What was happening? How could he just disappear? Suddenly, everything went dark again.

Chapter 23

Colt

I moped into the room and sensed something was wrong. Callie's face was twisted with a cross between confusion and fear, but her eyes remained closed. I took her hand in mine, and her face softened a little.

"Colt, don't leave me," she cried in a whisper that was barely audible.

"Callie, I'm right here. Open your eyes," I replied in a soft tone. I kissed her hand. "Please open your eyes," I pleaded, willing the tears not to fall.

"Any change?" Luke appeared in the doorway of her hospital room.

"I'm not sure. I thought she said something, but she didn't wake up, so I don't know if I only imagined it."

"Why don't you get some rest? I'll sit with her for a while."

"No." I growled.

Luke put his hands up and said, "Okay, okay. I'll check back later." He headed back out the doorway.

I just grunted in reply. How could they not understand that I couldn't leave her? What if she woke up, and I wasn't there?

Be still and know, My Son.

As soon as I heard those words, I bowed my head. I didn't

pray. I stayed silent, waiting on the Lord.

* * *

The next morning, Doc Mitchell came into the room. He checked Callie's vitals and her oxygen levels, and then her ankle. "Her body seems to be recovering, which is a good sign. The swelling has gone down significantly. I would say we should see her waking up in the next few hours. If there are any changes, call the nurse."

"Thanks, Doc. Will do."

When Doc Mitchell left the room, I grasped Callie's hand once more. That's the last thing I remembered.

My eyes opened when I felt Callie's hand twitch in mine. I must have fallen asleep. I had stayed up all night praying that she would be okay and wake up.

"Callie?" I popped up and leaned over the side of the bed.

She turned her head, and tears began to fall down her cheeks. "Why did you leave me? I couldn't find you. I was so scared."

"I never left ya, sweetheart. I've been right here the whole time." My heart thumped in my chest. I don't know if it was because of her tears or the fact she was awake to *have* tears.

"What happened? Where am I?" Callie's eyes darted around the room.

"Ya don't remember getting bit by a snake?" She shook her head. "Warrior came and got me, and then Jon and I brought ya to the hospital. Doc Mitchell said ya went unconscious because your body went into shock and because of your low blood pressure. He hooked ya up to an IV to give ya antivenom. Ya had me so worried. The guys told me Warrior has been beside himself. He won't leave the spot where I left him at the stable."

"How long was I unconscious?"

"It happened yesterday morning, but it felt like forever. Doc told me to call the nurse if ya woke up, so let me go get her."

"Okay."

I went to the doorway. "Nurse! She's awake."

As the nurse approached the door, I said, "Doc Mitchell told me to tell ya if anything changed."

"Thank you." The nurse entered the room and went to the machine keeping Callie's vitals. "How're ya feeling, Callie?"

"Thirsty, hungry, tired, sore."

"Well, let me call Doctor Mitchell, and we will see what we can do about any or all of those, okay?"

"Thank you."

"Thanks," I said as she passed me to leave. *Thank you, Lord, for bringing Callie back to me.*

"How's our patient?" Doc asked as he stepped into the room about fifteen minutes later. "Hi, Callie. I'm Doctor Mitchell. Do you mind if I take a look at you?"

Callie shook her head. "No, I don't mind."

"How're ya feelin'?"

"Thirsty, tired, hungry, sore, but other than that, I feel okay."

"Well, let's check to see how things are progressing here." He checked her breathing and heart rate, oxygen levels, her ears and eyes, and finally her ankle.

"Everything looks great. Swelling is continuing to go down. Vitals have improved significantly. I think you should be okay to be discharged this evening, but we will wait and see what things look like at that time, okay?"

"Okay." Callie said in a sullen tone. "Can I at least drink some water or something? Can I have food?"

"You can have fluids. Breakfast was already served, but if someone wants to bring you something, I won't object. Otherwise, it's Jell-O and popsicles until suppertime."

Callie groaned. She glanced at me with begging eyes.

I removed my phone from my pocket and stepped into the hall. How could I possibly resist those eyes? I called Aunt Marie, and she was more than willing to bring some sustenance for Callie. "Aunt Marie is bringing you something," I told Callie, stepping back into the room. I shoved my phone back in my pocket and returned to my seat at the bed.

"Thank you so much. I hate Jell-O." Callie opened her mouth and stuck out her tongue in disgust.

I chuckled and shook my head.

It wasn't long before Aunt Marie and Uncle Carl arrived. They were the calvary bringing the coveted food. "Hey there, sweetheart. How are you feeling?" Aunt Marie ushered me out of the way to reach Callie despite there being a whole other side of the bed available.

Callie scooted to a sitting-up position. "My mouth is watering because of the smells coming from that basket. Otherwise, I'm okay. Thank you both so much for coming."

Aunt Marie patted Callie's hand. "Of course, dear."

"Hi, Carl." Callie smiled over at him.

"So good to see you," he told her, setting the basket on the tray table at the foot of the bed.

"We won't stay. I'm sure you need your rest." Aunt Marie fussed. "Enjoy the goodies."

"Hand that basket over," Callie demanded with outstretched arms when Aunt Marie and Uncle Carl were out of sight.

I chuckled and dragged the tray table up to within her reach.

"Oooooh. She brought me banana muffins. My favorite." Callie took a bite, closed her eyes, and leaned back on the pillow. "So delicious." I went to grab a muffin for myself when she smacked my hand. She giggled. "I'm just kidding." She beamed at me.

"Thanks." I smiled at her and grabbed a muffin before she could smack my hand again.

We watched some TV, played some card games, and she slept to pass the time. I did enjoy watching her sleep. She didn't know it, but I was going to insist she stay at the house for a while after her discharge. I hoped she wouldn't put up a fight.

"Okay, Colt and Callie," Doc Mitchell announced his presence. "Your vitals have stayed steady in a good range, and I'm pleased with the amount the swelling has gone down. With the x-rays we took when you first arrived, it doesn't appear there is tissue damage, which is an excellent thing. I'm going to let you go home, but I suggest you have someone with you for a while in case things change. I want to see you in my office in about two to three weeks. If you are still in a great deal of pain, I will suggest physical therapy. Callie, you are going to have to take it easy for a while. No standing or walking for long periods of time, especially alone. Take Tylenol for the pain. Call me if you need me."

"Thank you, Doctor," Callie gave him a slight smile.

"The nurse will be in with your discharge paperwork shortly."

"Doctor, will I be able to take a shower at least?"

"I can help ya wash your hair," I chimed in without thinking about what I was saying. "In the sink. I can help ya wash your hair in the sink," I quickly corrected. The look of horror on Callie's face sent a surge of heat up my own. I wrapped my hand around the back of my neck and sighed.

Doc shook his head and chuckled. "My suggestion is you take a sponge bath. Just until you get your bearings back. Make sure you drink plenty of fluids."

"Okay." Callie stuck her bottom lip out again.

By the time we left the hospital, it was about 6 p.m.

"Do ya want to stop and get somethin' to eat, Callie?"

"Can you just take me home?"

"I'll take ya back to my house."

"No."

"You heard Doc. He said ya should have someone with ya for a while."

She sighed deeply. "Fine. Can we at least go to my cabin so I can get some clothes?"

"Sure."

We drove to the ranch in complete silence. It wasn't an awkward silence. I just didn't know what to talk about. Callie sat with her eyes closed and her head resting against the back of the seat. I didn't want to disturb her. I knew it was going to take some time to get back to normal. We stopped at her cabin so she could pack a bag. When we pulled up to my house, I helped her down and grabbed her bag from the back seat.

"You can stay in the master bedroom. It's downstairs and has its own bathroom."

"Thank you," Callie said softly.

"You're welcome."

"I'm going to take a . . . sponge bath, I guess." Callie sighed and rolled her eyes.

"Alright. I should probably get cleaned up myself."

As soon as I heard the bathroom door click, I ran upstairs. I took a quick shower and then headed down to the kitchen to find something to drink. Why did I tell her she was staying at my house? I growled loudly. No woman had stepped onto the property, let alone my house, not since . . . I didn't want to finish that thought. I sighed and ran my hand through my hair.

There was a clamor in the kitchen. I was startled to find Richard still there. My heart beat rapidly as I was expecting to be alone.

"Richard, you're still here?"

"Just prepping for breakfast. I was helping everyone with chores around the ranch, so I got behind on prepping the food. I barely had supper ready tonight."

"No worries. Thanks for steppin' up today. Just wasn't expectin' to find anyone here."

"Well, since I am, can I get ya anything?" Richard asked, wiping his hands on a towel.

"Stiff drink would be nice," I scoffed as I flopped down at the table.

"How about a cup of warm milk instead? Might help ya relax and get some sleep."

"Sure."

Richard smirked. "You've got it bad for her, don't ya?"

"Is it that obvious?"

He chuckled. "Only to those of us who have eyes." I set my head in my hands. "Have ya told her how ya feel?" Richard looked at me over the rim of his glasses.

I sighed deeply. "Kinda."

"What do you mean, 'kinda'?"

"I told her when she wasn't awake." I lifted my shoulders in a shrug and flashed a sheepish grin.

"Oh, Colt. You'd better tell that girl how ya feel, or someone else will come along and whisk her away."

"I know. I just don't know how. What if she doesn't feel the same? What if she runs away?"

"Ya won't know until ya tell her."

"I'm just terrified of getting into a relationship because of what Julia did to me. I don't know if I can truly trust a woman again, but Callie . . ." I ran my hands through my hair.

At the same time, Richard and I turned toward a noise in the hallway. We glanced at each other. Richard had a surprised expression that I knew I mirrored—eyes wide, mouth open. I closed my eyes and exhaled deeply. As I peeked around the corner into the hallway, Callie was hobbling away. Shoot! How much of the conversation had she heard? Since she was running—well limping—away, I guessed most of it.

"Callie, wait."

She paused but didn't turn around. "I need to go."

"What? Why? I'm guessin' ya heard our conversation?" I sighed.

"I'm sorry. I didn't mean to eavesdrop. I just wanted a glass of water." Her voice broke. "Good night, Colt." As fast as her limp would allow, she hurried out of sight.

"What just happened?" I whispered as I massaged the back of my neck.

Chapter 24

Callie

I tried to hold back tears as I hobbled to the bedroom. By the time I closed the door, my ankle was on fire. I flung myself on the bed and let the tears flood my face. How could I not see he didn't want a relationship, especially with me? He must have noticed I had a crush on him and didn't want to hurt my feelings. I was the friend the guy was friends with out of pity—to let the fat girl down easy. It happened all the time.

I felt so stupid for allowing myself to fall for Colt, but I felt even more stupid for hoping he felt the same way about me. I had wanted it to be true so badly that I didn't think about the reality that he didn't feel the same. I should have known better. My aunt's voice penetrated my mind, just like it always did, rubbing it in she was right. *Men don't like fat girls like you.* But why would he spend all that time at the hospital? Because he cares. *That doesn't mean he's in love with you.* I pulled at the hair on the sides of my head, hoping it would hush my aunt's voice. I was more confused than ever.

Why, God? Why do I always do this? When will I find a Godly man that will love me and want me? I just don't understand what I did that was so wrong that I would be punished like this.

I knew God didn't punish people like that, but it sure felt

like a punishment—perpetual solitary confinement is what it felt like to me. I was destined to be alone. I squeezed the pillow tightly against my body and sobbed into it until I had no tears left. I hadn't cried quite that hard since my parents died. I would have to grieve the loss of my best friend and then heal my broken heart. I just didn't see any other options.

Chapter 25

Colt

I lifted my hand to knock on the door, but I paused as Callie's cries pierced my ears. My chest constricted, the pain shot through my heart, and my arm fell to my side. I thought she felt the same way about me. I pressed my head to the door and sighed heavily. How had I gotten it so wrong? How could I be so stupid to think she felt that way about me? I wasn't anything special. At least, not enough to get her attention as anything other than friends. Hadn't Julia taught me that much? I wanted Callie to have feelings for me so much I didn't think about the reality she didn't. I would have to grieve the loss of my best friend.

God, what is so wrong with me that she doesn't want to be with me or love me? Am I not good enough for love? Am I destined to be alone?

I would just have to learn to put the wall back up around my heart so I could learn to not feel what I was feeling for her. I should have never let it come down in the first place. There wasn't anything more I could do. I glanced one last time at the closed door between us and retreated to my own room.

Chapter 26

Callie

I took my time getting up and dressed the next morning, but I wanted to make sure I made it to breakfast to ask Luke for a ride to my cabin. I just couldn't stay in the house, not when I knew he didn't want a relationship, especially one with me. I wasn't even sure I could stay in Edenton, much less at the ranch. Tears stung my eyes and threatened to fall. I inhaled, closed my eyes tight, and the tears retreated. At least at the cabin, I could breathe and think clearly. I limped and winced to the kitchen. When my presence in the room became known, conversation stopped, and all eyes were on me—all except for two. Colt never turned, never acknowledged my existence. His lack of acknowledgment stabbed me in the heart, removed the blade, and stabbed me again.

"Good morning." I plastered the best fake grin on my face I could.

"Mornin'," some said in unison, and others followed.

Colt's eyes never left his plate. When I sat down, his jaw clenched. Everyone passed platters full of sausage, eggs, and fried potatoes. I scooped very little onto my plate. I didn't have much of an appetite.

"Luke." I paused to steady my voice. "After breakfast, could you give me a ride back to my cabin, please?"

"Sure. No problem." He glanced at Colt with questions in his eyes.

Colt's eyes remained on his plate and gave no response.

"Thank you." My lip quivered. I moved my food around on the plate from side to side.

As the guys finished eating, they stood from the table and carried their dishes to the sink before heading out the door to complete their daily chores.

"Callie, are ya ready to go?" Luke asked after stacking his dishes in the sink.

"What?" I broke from my thoughts. "Oh. Yes. Thank you." I began to pick up my dishes.

"Just leave them," Colt barked.

"Okay." I slammed the dishes on the table, grabbed my bag from around the corner, and strolled out the door with Luke. I guess breaking my heart wasn't enough for him. He had to bark orders, too.

Once back at my cabin, I could breathe for the first time since leaving the security of the bedroom, but as much as I loved being here, I couldn't stay at Redemption Ranch any longer. If only I could take Warrior with me. As much as it broke my heart, I knew I needed to say goodbye to him. I shuffled over to the stable, my heart in my hands.

"Hey, boy!" I rubbed Warrior's nose, choking back the tears. "I'm going to have to leave. I'm so sorry," I whispered so no one but Warrior could hear. "If I could take you with me, I would. You continue to get strong. You're an amazing horse and an even better friend. I love you and will never forget you." I leaned into him, put my arms around his neck, and shed a few tears.

I let go of Warrior and limped away without ever glancing back. If I did, I wouldn't leave him, and I had to leave to save myself. As I trudged back to my cabin, I surveyed my general vicinity to see if anyone was close by, grabbed my phone out of my pocket, and called Olivia.

"Hey, Olivia."

"Hey, Cal. What's up? How're ya feelin'?"

"Depends. You asking mentally or physically?" I kicked at some rocks, fighting back the tears that threatened to spill. "Can I come stay with you? It obviously would be very temporary. Just until I can find my own place."

"What? Why? What happened?"

"I'll explain when I get there. I promise it won't be long." I cleared my throat, both to fight back my emotions and to calm my nerves.

"Of course, you can."

I breathed a sigh of relief. "Can I come now?"

"Yep. I'm off today."

"Thank you so much. See ya in a bit."

"I'll be waiting."

I put my phone back in my pocket and limped to the cabin. I need a little time to figure out a new direction for my life. Once again, I packed all my worldly possessions in my bags. One day, I hoped I'd find where I belonged and never have to pack my things up again. I thought it was this ranch. Wrong again. I put my bags in my Jeep and hobbled back inside to leave a note for whoever found the cabin empty. Even though Colt wasn't interested in a relationship or love, I knew he would worry. He couldn't help himself.

To Whom It May Concern,

I feel it's time for me to move on, so I have left the ranch. Thank you for everything you all have done for me and taught me, but I think it's best if I leave. I wish you all nothing but the best. I will never forget any of you. Please take care of Warrior for me.

All My Love,

Callie

I placed the letter on the kitchen table and put the key on top of it before shutting the door one final time. As I drove down the long lane, I peeked in the rearview mirror to take one last glance at the ranch. My heart shattered as a lonely tear escaped down my cheek.

Olivia was sitting on the front porch when I arrived.

"Hey," I greeted as I stepped onto the porch and winced.

"Hey there," Olivia said with her brows furrowed. "Are you okay? What happened? Wait. Let's get ya inside and settled first."

"Are you sure it's okay I stay with you?"

"Are ya kidding? You know Edna adores ya. Besides, I'm house-sitting for her and taking care of Mr. Wells, her cat, because her son and his family whisked her away on a family vacation in Florida."

As if on cue, Mr. Wells jumped onto the windowsill to see who had arrived. Olivia opened the door and ushered me inside. Mr. Wells rubbed against my leg.

"Well, hello, Mr. Wells. How are you?" I asked as I bent down and scooped him up. I was able to pet him a few times before he leaped down and sauntered away.

"You can take my room in the apartment. I'll sleep on the couch in here."

"Are you sure?"

"Yeah. It'll be fine." Olivia waved me off.

I limped after Olivia into her apartment, which had its own

door on the inside of the house. Her apartment, she had told me, was either a maid's quarters or in-law quarters back when the house was built. I dropped my bags on the bed, and my heart became so heavy. I sat down, laid my head in my hands, and began to cry. I didn't want to or mean to, but I couldn't hold the tears in.

"Callie, tell me what's wrong," Olivia begged as she knelt in front of me.

"He isn't interested in a relationship. He doesn't know if he can trust a woman. So, there's really no hope." My bottom lip quivered and stuck out farther than my top one.

"Oh, honey. I don't think that's true."

"I heard it with my own ears."

"Okay. I would suggest we take a walk, but your ankle . . . Why don't ya go take a shower? It will help ya relax a little. Then, we can sip some hot chocolate on the back porch, and you can tell me everything."

"Okay."

I didn't have the energy to argue. My ankle was raging. Weariness overcame me, and I just wanted to sleep. In an attempt to calm myself and rest my ankle before taking a shower, I laid back on the bed and closed my eyes. The last thing I heard was a knock at the door.

Chapter 27

Colt

I inhaled and exhaled deeply before putting my fist to Olivia's door. Reading Callie's note that morning made my heart break into a million pieces. "Hey, Olivia. Is she here?" I asked when the door opened.

"She's sleeping," she whispered, stepping out onto the porch and closing the door.

I ran my hands through my hair and massaged the back of my neck. "I can't figure out what I did wrong." Tears stung my eyes. I was so confused about my feelings for Callie and how those feelings were affecting me in a way I had never known. I had never shed tears for a woman in my life, not even when Julia left me. I just didn't understand.

"She thinks you will never want a relationship with her because you don't trust women or something like that."

"What? How could she possibly? Oh, she heard my conversation with Richard." I was more confused than before. I sighed as it dawned on me the part of the conversation Callie must have focused on. "That wasn't about *her*, though. How do I convince her I felt that way *before* she came along?"

"That, my friend," Olivia started as she placed her hands on my shoulders, "is something you have to figure out on your own."

I groaned. "Okay. Her birthday is next week. I've already got somethin' planned. I'll do my best to give her space until then. I just hope I can survive."

I was being somewhat melodramatic, but I had gotten used to Callie being around every day. It was going to be an adjustment not having her by my side. She had become my best friend over the last three months. Her absence was going to leave a huge gap in my heart and in my life. Warrior was going to feel it, also—of that, I was sure. I let Olivia in on my plan.

"Will ya help me, please?"

"I'll try, Colt, but I can't make her do anything she doesn't want to do. I will do my best to convince her, though."

"That's all I can ask. Thank you." I kissed her cheek before bolting to my truck.

This had to work. *Please, God, let this work. I need this to work.* I was thankful it was a grief group night. I doubted Callie would be there, but I sure hoped she would show up. In the meantime, I had a lot of work to do. The Harvest Festival was in a couple of weeks. I was going to have to wrangle up more help since I lost my planning partner. We had gotten a majority of the planning done, but there was still more left to do.

Once back at the ranch, I hustled through my chores. I needed to be done in time to help Jon set up for the meeting. I mindlessly fed the horses and dropped hay in their stalls. I didn't completely muck out the stalls but shoveled the manure that was causing the vomit-inducing stench. When I stopped at Warrior's space, he was pacing and stomping.

"I know, boy. I miss her, too." I lifted my hand to pet his nose, but he shied away. "Are we back to *that* now? Not letting anyone touch ya? Not even a little? I sure hope my plan for Callie works."

My shoulders slumped with sadness for Warrior. For me.

My heart squeezed as if it was in a vice grip. It was grieving once more, except this time, it was for the woman who had managed to steal it. *God, this can't be it for us. Whatever is in Your will for us, so be it. I will honor You and glorify You no matter what. I love you, Lord.* I started working on fixing a door to one of the empty stalls as it wouldn't come close to latching. It needed new hinges. Now seemed as good a time as any to fix it.

"Are ya ready to go?" Jon asked, sauntering into the stable.

"Is it time already? I feel like I just started." I wiped my brow with my arm. I guess I did get started later than usual because I chased after Callie. "Give me a couple of minutes to finish up and put my tools away." I glanced down at my clothes. "Guess I should get washed up and changed, too."

"I'll meet ya at your house."

"Okay." I sighed.

God, please let my plan work. I closed my eyes and stood in silence for just a moment, just to breathe. The next week was going to be torture. If my plan didn't work, it was going to destroy me. That scared me like nothing else ever had. I shook my head clear, secured my tools in my toolbox, and with my heavy heart, headed to my house.

It wasn't long before Jon and I were in the truck and heading to the library. I dropped Jon off to set up while I picked up refreshments. When Jon shut the door, I headed up Broad Street to Courageous Café and Bakery. As soon as the bells jingled, signaling I was inside, I knew she was there. I didn't even have to see her to know. I scanned the café, trying to be inconspicuous. I spotted Callie at a table by the window with Olivia.

I nodded to Olivia before moseying to the counter. I wanted so badly to go to Callie. As soon as the thought left my mind, Exodus 14:14 swept in. *The Lord will fight for you, and you have only to be silent.* I closed my eyes and thanked God for the reassurance.

I opened my eyes just as Dylan came to the counter to ring me up. Because I had grown up with Marci and Chuck, and we were all such close friends, I considered their kids to be my niece and nephew. If I could have aspired to have the faith and love of anyone, it would be the Logan family. Marci and Chuck were high school sweethearts and got married. Then, they had two beautiful kids. They bought the café from Chuck's parents when they wanted to retire. Marci and Chuck revamped it into Courageous Café and Bakery. I was expecting to see Caitlyn at the counter as she was usually the one there.

"Hey, Dyl. I'm here to pick up my order. Where's Caitlyn?"

"Well, hi to you, too, Uncle Colt." He laughed before he turned somber. "Caitlyn's at home. Blood sugar has been low the last day or so."

"Aww. I'm sorry to hear that. Please tell her I said hi and give her a hug for me?"

"Will do," Dylan told me as he passed the box of pastries across the counter. "See ya next time."

"Thanks, Dyl. See ya next time." I tipped my hat to him in a nod.

I turned and peered in Callie's direction. I couldn't help myself. She glanced up, and our eyes met. I tried to smile as much as I could muster in the moment, but it fell short. I didn't want to break my gaze, but I bowed my head and strode out the door.

Chapter 28

Callie

"**W**hy don't ya talk to him, Callie?" Olivia asked over the buzzing of other patrons in the café.

"I can't. At least, not right now. I have to learn to accept things the way they are and move forward." I glanced down at my hands folded in my lap.

"You're not leaving Edenton, are ya?"

"I honestly don't know. I don't want to, but it's a small town, and I'm not sure I can handle seeing him and not being able to be *with* him." I laced the white cotton material of the tablecloth between my fingers, attempting to calm my nerves after Colt strode out of the café. I pictured myself throwing the small glass vase holding the pretty, colorful flowers against the wall. That's what I really wanted to do.

"Oh, Callie." Olivia put her hands on mine after I laid them on the table.

I shrugged and tried to smile. I knew if I left, I would be opening a wound I had been trying so hard to close. I would have to grieve the loss of yet another family. When Olivia left the table to use the restroom, I decided to pray. *God, I don't know what to do. My heart is so heavy, Lord. Please don't forsake me! Show me the way. Show me Your will. Whatever it is, I will love You and glorify You always. Amen.* I opened my eyes to find Olivia's staring back at me.

"Sorry." My cheeks became warm.

"No worries. I just didn't wanna interrupt ya. We should probably get ya back to the house and off that ankle." Olivia nodded toward the door.

"Do you think you could drop me off at the library? I really could use grief group tonight." I glanced around the café and stopped at the writing on the wall. *BE STRONG AND COURAGEOUS.* I didn't need to read the rest. I lifted my chin and stood from the table. "I'm ready." I said it with more confidence than I knew I possessed and hobbled to the door.

I sucked in some crisp country air before climbing into Olivia's older model, green VW Beetle. I played with the little fabric flower she kept in the cup holder. Her car always smelled like I was lost in a field of wildflowers. I leaned my head against the headrest and closed my eyes, trying to calm my nerves before I came face-to-face with Colt again. I had to do this. I needed to. If I was going to stay there without him, I had to be able to see him and be in the same room without losing it. That night would be good practice. It would be complete torture on my heart but good practice.

"Wish me luck."

Olivia hopped out to drag me into a hug before I gimped inside. "Good luck. Call me when you're ready to be picked up."

I entered the library. I placed my hand on the handle to the room, took a deep breath in, exhaled, and willed my feet to move and my hand to open the door. Once inside, I scanned the room until my eyes fell on Colt. His back was to me, but the effect was still the same. My lungs were unable to take in air. He was still the most beautiful man I had ever laid my eyes on. I wondered if he would always have that effect on me, especially when there was a possibility I would see him with another woman that wasn't me. At that thought, I felt a sharp pang in my chest. I would just have to live a life of heartache and pain, *if* I wanted to stay in Edenton.

Chapter 29

Colt

I knew the minute she stepped into the room. Goosebumps formed on my arms, and my chest tingled—just like it did every time she was near. Would she always have that effect on me? She would know soon enough how I truly felt about her, and I hoped to know her feelings for me, too.

"Okay, everyone. Let's take our seats," Jon belted out over the loud group.

I took my seat, my leg jiggling with nervous energy as I was about to do something I never had before. I was going to be vulnerable. Everyone in the room knew how my dad died. Everyone but her. I wanted her to know—no, I *needed* her to know. I hated being vulnerable, but I had already decided if she showed up, I was going to tell my story.

"Who'd like to share first?" Jon asked.

"I will," I spoke up as I raised my hand.

Jon's face flashed concern. "Are you sure?"

I nodded.

"Okay. Go ahead."

I inhaled and exhaled. "As most of ya know, my dad passed away four years ago on August 8th," I started as I stared at my twisted hands. It was still so hard for me to talk about. "Most of ya also know how he died. He was working on harvesting the sweet corn in our fields." I paused. I had never actually talked about his death before. I avoided it at all costs. "We had a tractor-pulled harvester. Ya know my dad. He never wanted the most up-to-date equipment if he didn't have to have it." A chuckle barely passed my lips. "At some point, my dad had a heart attack and fell off the back of the tractor, and the harvester ran over him." I heard my voice crack, and the tears began to form as I remembered seeing him lying there. "I found him in the field."

I swiped at my eyes. I glanced up at Callie, expecting to see pity in her eyes, but what I saw were tears, compassion, and understanding, and that gave me the courage to continue. "The medical examiner said, luckily, he passed before he hit the ground, so he went quickly and didn't feel what the harvester had done to his body. I'm not sure I'll ever get that image out of my head, and I feel like I fail his legacy and memory every day." I covered my face with my hands.

Jon placed his hand on my back. "Why don't we take a break?"

Once everyone was busy getting refreshments, Jon whispered, "Go get a breath of fresh air. I'll send someone out to get ya when we're ready to start again."

I just nodded. I didn't trust my voice in that moment. My vision blurred as I hurried from the room and the stares that were burning into me. Once I reached the curb, I took a deep breath. I hadn't planned on talking or saying as much as I did, but Callie was there. She needed to know I understood at least some of her pain. I ran my hand through my hair and squeezed the back of my neck before stuffing my hands in my front pockets. My spirit felt lighter. I didn't realize the amount of grief I had been holding inside for the last four years. I sighed deeply. She needed to be in my arms. Then, as if on cue, she

147

was there. I still wasn't sure how I always knew she was there before she said anything.

"Colt," she said softly as she touched my arm. "Are you okay?"

I turned to open my mouth to say yes, but instead, I pulled her into my arms and held on. The tears poured down my cheeks before I could stop them. I wanted to tell Callie that I desperately wanted to be in a relationship with her and that I was in love with her, but I knew if I did, she would run, and she felt too good in my arms to let her go.

"We should probably get back inside," Callie said, stepping out of my embrace.

"Yeah. Okay." I ran my hand through my hair. I shivered because she took the warmth with her. "Hey, if ya need a ride after, let me know."

"Olivia is coming to pick me up but thank you." She avoided my gaze and turned to go back inside.

My heart fell to the pit of my stomach. I sighed. I just stood there for a few minutes staring up at the sky. I shoved my hands in my pockets. *Lord, help me get through this.* I trudged back into the library to support the others in the group. When the meeting drew to a close, sadness invaded me. I didn't want the meeting to end because I knew, after that night, I might not see Callie again until her birthday, and that was *if* Olivia could convince her. Could I live with that? The hole in my heart screamed I could not.

The meeting dispersed, and I helped clean up. I wanted to say good night to Callie, but she had already gone. I stacked the last chair in its proper place. Where was *my* proper place? If Callie continued to live here but rejected my affection, could I remain in Edenton, ripping my heart apart every time I bumped into her? If it was God's will, I would. But oh, how I hoped it wasn't.

"Jon, ya ready to go?"

"Yep," he responded, gathering his things and heading out the door.

I flipped off the lights, the darkness hiding the stinging tears trickling down my cheeks.

Chapter 30

Callie

I needed to clear my head, so I thought I would walk back to Olivia's house. It didn't seem that far from the library. Halfway there, though, excruciating pain shot through my ankle. I sat down on a nearby bench. *God, I don't know if I can do this. I don't know if I can see him all the time and know I'm not good enough to be with him. Even if he did love me, once he saw my scars, he would run and run quickly.*

My heart wrenched with pain. I covered my face with my hands, and my shoulders began to shake from the sobs. Why did he have to hug me like that? He felt so good in my arms. My heart ached for what he went through with his dad. Finding his dad like that must have been horrific. It made me thankful I didn't see my parents' dead bodies. I could remember them the way they were when they were alive.

"Callie?" A familiar voice called out.

I stood and hobbled over to the car. "Oh, hi, Marci. How are you?"

"I'm blessed. The better question is, how are *you*?"

"Well, after grief group, I decided to get some fresh air and walk back to Olivia's, but my ankle is screaming at me that it was a stupid idea." I did that thing where I half giggled and half groaned.

"Get in. I'll give ya a ride."

"Oh, I couldn't impose like that." My cheeks began to heat.

"Callie, if it were an imposition, I wouldn't have offered. Now. Get. In."

I opened the door and slid into the passenger seat of her maroon Dodge Durango. Black raspberry vanilla filled the air inside. I inhaled deeply. It smelled so sweet. In the months I had gotten to know Marci, I knew she was the type of person who would do anything for anyone, hence the ride home. The whole Logan family was that way. It was one of the many things I had grown to love about them.

"So, what's wrong?"

I crossed my arms. "Nothing."

"Callie." Marci peered at me out of the corner of her eye.

I sighed. She wouldn't give up until I talked.

"I'm just so confused. I heard Colt say he doesn't want to be in a relationship, and he doesn't know if he can trust women, but then some things he does make me wonder. Maybe I'm just reading too much into it. We're just friends. Well, we *were*."

Marci craned her neck. "Perhaps you didn't hear all the conversation?"

"I heard enough," I mumbled.

"Honey, I have known Colt his whole life, and I have never seen him look at a woman the way he looks at you."

"Really? I'm not so sure. Why would he be in love with me?" My lip quivered.

Marci tried but failed to stifle a giggle. "Why *wouldn't* he? I'd like to pray with you. I'd like to pray for God to give you the eyes to see you how He sees you. How Colt sees you. Can I do that?"

"Yes. That would mean a lot," I told her as she pulled up to the curb outside Olivia's place.

We joined hands and bowed our heads. "Father, God, You said where two or three are gathered in Your name, there You will be. We humbly come to You and ask that You help Callie to see herself how You see her—fearfully and wonderfully made. Guide her in the way You want her to go. Heal her heart, Father, and open it to the love You have for her life, whether it's romantic love, friendship love, family love, or all of the above. Your will be done, Father, God. Amen."

"Amen. Thank you, Marci. For the prayer and the ride."

"Anytime, Callie."

I slipped out of the car and limped my way inside.

"Callie?" Olivia asked, coming around the corner, eyes wide, a confused expression stamped on her face. "You were supposed to call me to pick you up. I about beaned ya with this bat." She held up an aluminum baseball bat.

"I know. I just needed some air, so I decided to walk. I stopped to rest because my ankle was hurting, and Marci saw me and offered me a ride."

"Callie, why did ya walk home?" Olivia stood in front of me with her hands on her hips. "Ya shouldn't be on your ankle. Doctor's orders."

I sighed. What could I say? She was right, but I wasn't about to tell her that. "I just need to lie down, ice my ankle, and fall asleep. I'm just mentally drained."

I started to wander off to bed. My ankle buckled. Olivia raced to my side and helped me slide under the covers into bed.

"I'll get you some ice," Olivia stated after I was settled.

As she came back in the room, Olivia was in mid-sentence. ". . . can't avoid living to avoid Colt, Callie . . ."

I didn't want to hear any more about Colt. I had enough to digest from the meeting, his story, and what happened outside the library. I pretended I was asleep. Once Olivia left the room, my mind wandered to why I had been so tired since coming to Edenton. I should be so well-rested. Again, maybe it was just dealing with all of the grief I never let go of. Maybe it had been weighing me down, and now that it is expelling from my body, I was just exhausted. The last thoughts I remembered having that night were of Colt. Oh, how I wanted a future with him.

Chapter 31

Colt

I shot straight up in bed, sweat dripping down my face, my heart racing, my body trembling. Ever since I talked about my dad's death last week in group, I had been having nightmares. I rubbed my hands up and down my face before slipping out of bed and heading to the kitchen to get a glass of water.

I sat at the kitchen table as the hug I shared with Callie flashed through my mind. I hadn't seen her since group, just like I had worried. It felt like it had been a lifetime since I had held her. She belonged in my life, in my arms. She felt so perfect there, like home. I needed her to be there with Warrior and me. I glanced at the clock—4 a.m. If I tried to go back to sleep, the dreams would return. Since I had so much to accomplish, I decided to take a quick shower, grab a bite, and head out. I wanted to get work done so I could make everything as perfect as possible for Callie on her birthday the next day. Olivia had convinced Callie to go out.

When I entered the stable, my first stop was Warrior's stall. Since Callie left, he went back to being withdrawn and wouldn't let anyone touch him. He barely let me touch him.

"I know, boy. It's all my fault. I'm hoping I can make it right tomorrow. I've got to make it right." I sighed and touched my forehead to the side of Warrior's face. "I guess I'd better

154

get to it. See ya later, Warrior boy."

I took Beauty out of her stall and saddled her up to go check the fence line. Taking Beauty out for a ride and checking the fence was my favorite thing to do. I loved it because it gave me the chance to get away from everyone. To keep my mind away from Callie, I put my earbuds in and hit play on my phone. I didn't have much confidence the music would work. Beauty and I trotted along the fence line. For once, nothing seemed to be in need of repair. On our way back to the stable, I ran Beauty at a full-out gallop. I loved the feeling of becoming one with her, and the wind in my face. Like always, it made me feel so free, especially when my heart was so heavy.

Once we returned to the stable, I led Beauty and the rest of the horses into the corral so I could muck out their stalls. As time drew near for me to begin setting up for the next day, my anxiety reached a level I hadn't experienced in years. I continued to pray to God that I wouldn't screw it up.

As soon as the horses were back in their stalls and their buckets filled with food, I headed over to the house for lunch and to recruit helpers. To my disbelief, everyone offered to help. Richard volunteered to plan a special meal. The others and I went to the old barn and hung lights and set up a table and chairs complete with a beige tablecloth and flower centerpiece. I placed a radio at the front of the room. Because everyone helped out, decorations were done in no time. I scanned the room and became overwhelmed with emotion. *God, please let this work.* I had never wanted an answered prayer more than this one. At that point, all I could do was wait.

Chapter 32

Callie

Olivia barged into the room. "Callie, are ya ready to go?"

I tugged at the hem of my dress. "Why do I have to wear a dress?" I didn't really like dresses. I wore one before because I was having dinner with Colt. Not to mention, it was always so hard to get the sizing right. If I bought one my size, it fit too tight, making me feel like a sausage stuffed in its casing. But one too big, I was in a muumuu.

"Because it's a special occasion, and ya look beautiful."

I turned to see myself in the mirror and did a double-take. Something was different. Pride surged through me. I felt beautiful. I grinned as Marci's prayer floated through my mind. Was this how God saw me? How Colt saw me? I didn't really know for sure, but I liked how *I* saw me.

"Ya also have to wear this." Olivia giggled, holding up a bandana.

I rolled my eyes. "Seriously? What am I, twelve? Are we playing Pin the Tail on the Donkey or something?"

Olivia shook with laughter. "I was given strict instructions. Now, turn so I can put it on you."

"By whom?"

"If I told ya, I would have to kill ya, or I would be killed. Either way, it'd be bad. Now, turn." She twirled her finger.

"And you expect me to trust you to guide me to the car?"

"Yes." Olivia huffed, spinning me around. She tied the blindfold over my eyes. "Can ya see anything?"

"No, and that terrifies me."

"Oh, stop. Let's go. Slow and steady. I promise I won't let ya trip or fall." She guided me to the car. Time seemed to stand still—aside from Olivia's driving.

"Olivia! Are you trying to make me puke? I'm already a bundle of nerves. My stomach doesn't need your help."

She cackled. "Sorry. Just trying to get ya there."

"Where are we going?"

"We already had this discussion."

A few minutes later, I sighed. "Are we there yet?"

"Almost. *Now*, you're sounding twelve."

Where were we going? I was tossed to and fro just before Olivia slowed to a stop. I immediately ripped off the blindfold before Olivia killed the engine. An old rustic barn I didn't recognize stood in front of me. I glanced in every direction.

"Where are we? Who's inside?" My palms began to sweat, and a shiver trickled down my spine.

"Go find out."

I stood from the car. Lights shimmered inside the barn. The area seemed familiar, but I couldn't figure out for the life of me why. A slight breeze brought with it the scent of magnolia trees. Was this on the ranch? It was the only place in Edenton I smelled those.

I took a deep breath. "Okay. Wish me luck."

"Good luck!" Olivia called after me.

I limped inside the barn. My breath caught in my throat. I hadn't seen anything like it. Who would go to all this trouble just for me? Twinkle lights were strung everywhere—over the door, hanging from the small platform at the front of the barn, strung from the beams in the ceiling. It was as if I was in a fairytale. A small table sat in the center of the barn with China plates and wine glasses, candles, and a flower centerpiece of white roses and baby's breath. I stared at the back of the man standing at the radio. I almost didn't recognize it was Colt. He turned around wearing a navy-blue suit. He was absolutely gorgeous. *Just breathe, Callie.* I exhaled.

When I found my voice, I let my confusion out with my words. "Colt, what are you doing here? What's going on? What is all this?" I lifted my arms slightly, looking in every direction.

Colt turned on the radio, a slow song. He sauntered over to me. "It's your birthday." He grinned. "And I made a promise to myself that I would do everything in my power to make your first birthday in Edenton as special as I could. Dance with me?" He held out his hand.

I brushed my clammy hands on the sides of my dress before laying one hand in his. I was so confused. Why would he do all of this? We came together as the lead singer of Rascal Flatts belted out the first line of "Bless the Broken Road." He sang about hoping to find true love on his journey, and he couldn't see that everything led to one woman. I rested my head on Colt's chest and got lost in my dreams of him being mine. As the song continued, I basked in the moment. I could get used to being wrapped in his arms, but he didn't love me or want a relationship. I didn't see any harm, though, in pretending for a while. It *was* my birthday, after all.

"I love you, Callie."

"What?" I asked, not sure if I had heard him correctly, stunned at his confession. I moved out of his arms and away from the magic of the moment.

"I've been mesmerized by you since the moment I saw ya in the Bistro when ya first got here. The more time we've spent together, the more I've fallen in love with you. That conversation ya heard me having with Richard, you must not have heard the whole thing. I said I didn't trust women or want a relationship, but then you came along and changed everything. Or at least that is what I was going to say until you bumped into the table in the hall. We're meant to be together, Callie. Please tell me I'm not imagining the connection between us. Please tell me you feel it, too."

The words I had longed to hear from him suddenly were strangling me. I was terrified. Everything my aunt ever beat into me came flooding in, and before I could stop it, her words were spewing from my mouth.

"Don't say that."

"Why not?" His voice crackled, and his face expressed pain.

I turned away from him. "Because you don't mean it. Men never do."

In that instant, my dream from the night Colt first kissed me floated into my mind. I realized that moment was my dream coming true. How could that be? Before I knew what was happening, Colt spun me around to face him and kissed me with a passion I had never known to exist. After he broke the kiss, he whispered breathlessly, "*Now*, tell me I don't mean it."

Tears formed in the corners of my eyes, and my breath caught in my throat again. I had to get out of there. I couldn't think or breathe, so I ran . . . well hobbled as quickly as I possibly could. Olivia was still outside. She was deep in conversation with Jon. I breathed a sigh of relief.

"Olivia," I hollered. "Let's go!"

"What? Why?"

"Let's go!" I snapped again before slamming the car door closed.

"What happened?" she asked as she put the key in the ignition.

"Please just drive," I begged her, pressing my hands into a praying position.

"Okay, but talk to me. Tell me what happened." Olivia stared, her eyes boring into my soul—a place I couldn't afford to let her into even though she was my best friend.

"I don't even know. I just need to think, to sort it out." I lowered my gaze. Confusion swirled in my head, my thoughts a jumbled mess.

Olivia sighed and started the engine. "Okay."

"Why didn't you tell me he is in love with me?" I craned my neck to look at her, slapping my hands against my legs.

"Cal, I wanted to so badly, but it wasn't my place to tell you. Besides, if I had, you would have just shrugged it off and not believed me."

I slammed my head against the back of the seat and let out a frustrated growl. "Probably right."

Questions and thoughts swam around in my head. *What just happened? Why did I run? Weren't those the words I so desperately wanted him to say to me?* An image of Colt, his face distorted with pain, slammed into my chest, causing my heart to ache. I leaned my head against the back of the seat and closed my eyes. What is wrong with me? In that moment, I hated myself. Hated my lack of confidence. Hated my inability to allow anyone to care for me. And he was right there, offering me the one thing I believed I would never deserve. Love. I balled my hands into fists and bit into my bottom lip. *Stupid, stupid girl!*

Chapter 33

Colt

"**W**hat just happened?" I whispered to myself as I ran my hand through my hair and scratched the back of my neck.

Confusion smashed into me. A deep pain settled right in the center of my chest. A frustrated scream escaped. Unfortunately, it didn't make me feel any better. I needed advice, and I knew exactly where to go. I jumped into my truck and peeled out, throwing dirt and rocks behind me. My knuckles were white from my grip on the steering wheel, my emotions getting the best of me.

When I arrived at the Logan farm, I inhaled and found Chuck on the front lawn. I parked to the side of their log home. It was a deep brown. Marci had planted flowers around the perimeter. A memory garden rested on one side for all those family members who had passed. Chuck's dogs, one black and tan, one black and white, and the smallest all white, ran to greet me. Chuck held a tennis ball in his hand.

"Hey, Colt," Chuck called out, strolling over to meet me.

"Hey, Chuck. I was wonderin' if I could bend your ear if ya have a minute."

"Sure. Let's go have a seat." He motioned toward the porch. "So, what's goin' on?"

We sat on the steps, and I proceeded to tell him what had

transpired between Callie and me.

"She sure is keepin' you on your toes, isn't she?"

"Yeah. I just don't know what to do. Do I go after her? Do I wait and see what happens? I'm just terrified she's going to leave town."

"Give her some time. She has to figure out things on her own. Maybe she is just as terrified as you are. Seems she has trouble trustin' people. From what I know of her life before she got here, I can't say I blame her. If it's in God's will for the two of you to be together, He will make it so. You just have to be patient. His timin' is not our timin'. I know that's probably not what you wanted to hear, but I hope it helps."

"Yeah." I sighed. "I know you're right. It's just goin' to be difficult to wait. But I guess I've waited this long." I stood up. "Guess I should get back to the ranch and clean up and let ya get back to what ya were doing. Thanks for the talk, Chuck; I appreciate it."

"No problem. Any time. Let me know how things work out."

I already knew Chuck would find out without my having to say anything. Small towns worked that way. After I left the Logan farm, I made my way over to the cemetery to talk things out with my dad. It was times like these that made me miss him even more.

I traveled down the old dirt road on the outskirts of town to my dad's burial site. The trees that lined the road swayed in the light breeze. I arrived at the cemetery and trotted over to the stone marker that bared my last name. The cemetery was always pristine. The caretaker made sure the lawn was always mowed and dead flowers were removed from graves. I sat down, bent my legs, and rested my elbows on my knees.

"Hey, Daddy. I know it's been a while since I've been

here. I miss you terribly. I desperately need your help . . . I met this amazin' woman. Her name is Callie, but as usual, I messed it all up. Ya know how I am with women . . . I don't really know how, but I messed up royally. Maybe she doesn't feel the same way about me. Maybe I got it all wrong. I just don't know what to do to fix it. Or if it can even be fixed at all. I wish ya were here to tell me what to do."

I sat there for a while staring at my dad's name etched into the marble stone, trying to think of what he would tell me if we were sitting at the old dining room table where most of our "man-to-man" talks took place.

"I miss you so much, Daddy. I hope I am makin' ya proud and not disappointed. I know I'm not runnin' the ranch how you did or how you taught me, but I think what I'm doin' is helpin' so many people, or at least, I hope it is. Anyway, I know if you were here, ya'd tell me that I've told her how I feel, and I should just give her some space and wait for her to come to me. Yeah, that's what Chuck Logan said, too."

Deep down, I wanted to run to her and convince her that I love every part of her, inside and out, but with a woman like her, it had to be her decision. She'd already experienced too much of people telling her what she needed to do and so much more. I kissed my fingertips and ran them over my dad's name, the cold, rough stone registering through my calloused skin.

"Thanks for listenin'." I stood and strode over to my truck. I shifted it into drive while shifting my heart into neutral. As badly as I wanted to make it happen, all I could do was keep my heart open. That scared me more than anything. Callie held the power to destroy me or make me the happiest man on Earth. The problem was, I had no idea which way it would go. Turning up the music as loud as it would go, I pressed down on the gas pedal and floored it to the ranch.

Chapter 34

Callie

I sat at a table in Courageous Café, staring at the scripture painted on the wall while sipping my hot chocolate. *BE STRONG AND COURAGEOUS.* I began to question what that even meant. I just didn't know anymore. Wasn't I strong enough since my parents had died? I was tired of always being strong. When Colt said he was in love with me, all I wanted to do was melt into his arms, but all my self-doubt, my self-hate spewed from inside me. I didn't want to acknowledge it, but my aunt was in my head, just like she always was, and I didn't know how to stop it. My head fell forward so my chin hit my chest. What was I supposed to do? Could I fix it somehow? Or was it too late?

"Hey, Callie. Happy birthday. How was the cake?" Marci asked, approaching the table.

I lifted my head. "What cake?"

"Oh no! I hope I didn't ruin the surprise. Caitlyn and I made a cake for you. Colt picked it up this morning."

Of course, he did. He tried so hard to give me a perfect birthday, and I couldn't get past my own demons. I grimaced. "You didn't. *I* did."

"What do ya mean? What happened?" She sat down across from me.

"Colt told me he's in love with me, and I freaked out. I told him he didn't mean it, and then he kissed me."

"What did you do?"

"I ran like a coward." I closed my eyes. "I don't even know what to do now. How do I fix it? *Can* I fix it?"

"Do you feel the same about him?"

"Yes. It just scares me . . . a lot. I've been hurt so much in my life, physically and mentally. I trust him with my whole heart, but how do I get my head to be on the same page as my heart?" I peered into Marci's eyes, searching for help, for answers, as tears streamed down my cheeks. She handed me a napkin to wipe my tears.

"Do you know that God tells us to not fear in one way or another 365 times in the Bible?"

"Wow. No. I didn't know that."

"I see the way you two look at each other and how you are when you are together. I don't think I've ever seen Colt as happy as he is when he's with you. The whole town feels that way, really. Do you feel Colt is who God has for you?"

"I think so," I responded, softer than I intended.

"Then you need to be strong and courageous." Marci motioned toward the wall. "You need to tell him how you feel. He deserves to know. You both deserve to be happy, even if you don't think you do. I know for a fact Colt wouldn't have said those words if he didn't mean them."

"Really? But what if he doesn't forgive me?"

"If he truly loves you, forgiveness won't be an issue." She nodded as if to convince me she was right. "Now, go tell that man you love him."

For the second time since arriving in Edenton, I heard that voice say, *you can't step out into the fullness of the Light with one foot stuck in the darkness. You have to let go of past hurts and truly forgive those who caused them. Not just a sound bite but the forgiveness that comes from deep within. From Me.* A lightbulb went off in my head. I knew exactly what I needed to do.

"There's something I have to do first. Thank you, Marci." I stood from the table and limped out the door. I drove to Olivia's and packed a bag. She was at work, so I left her a note.

Olivia,

There's something I have to do. I have to go out of town for a few days. I'll talk to you when I get back.

Love,

Callie

I threw my bag on the passenger seat and started the Jeep. In order to get my aunt out of my head and move forward with Colt, I had to forgive her. It was a long drive, but I had to do it. My future depended on it. Love depended on it. *Colt* depended on it.

When I arrived in Indianapolis, it was too early in the morning to go to my aunt's, so I went to a nearby restaurant to wait out the time. It was a small mom-and-pop place on the outskirts of the city. It was one of the only restaurants open twenty-four hours every day.

God, help me to find the words, strength, and courage. I know I have to do this. For myself. For Colt. Guard my heart, Father. Amen.

After a few hours, I inhaled and exhaled deeply before leaving the restaurant. I worked hard to calm my nerves. My palms were clammy. I hadn't seen my aunt since I turned eighteen. When I stopped in front of her house, the memories flooded in—the beatings, the berating, everything. I closed my eyes and asked God to silence the memories and to flood my mind with the words He wanted me to say.

"Here goes," I said to myself before stepping onto the pavement and trekking up to the door.

"What are you doing here? I thought I told you . . ." Aunt Carla started in as soon as she saw me standing at the door.

"Aunt Carla, I know what you told me. But I have something to say. I don't know what happened to you in your past to make you be so cruel. You beat me. You berated me. And I did *nothing* to deserve it. I came here not to bring up the past but to tell you that God loves you. He loves you with an unconditional love like no other, and . . . I forgive you. I forgive you with everything that is in me. Not for you. But for me. So I can move forward with my life instead of constantly living in the past. I hope one day you can find it in your heart to forgive, both those who have hurt you as well as yourself. I hope one day you accept Christ into your heart and accept the love He has for you because it is the most wonderful thing in the world. I also wanted to let you know you were wrong. There is a man who loves me. He is amazing, and now I'm going to drive away from here and never look back. Only forward to the life God has for me. Goodbye, Aunt Carla."

I glanced at my aunt as I turned to go. There were so many emotions in her expression, but what I saw most was confusion and sadness. For the first time in my life, I saw a single tear trickle down her cheek. I truly don't know what happened in her life that made her the way she was, but I hoped, one day, with the help of God, she could overcome her demons and find happiness in forgiveness before it was too late. I raced as quickly as my ankle would allow back to my Jeep and drove away. I never peered back. I kept moving forward and couldn't wait to get back to Colt, Warrior, and Edenton—my forever home.

Chapter 35

Colt

"What do ya mean she's not here?" I asked Olivia when she told me Callie had left. "Where'd she go?"

"I don't know. She left me a note saying there was something she had to do, so she would be gone for a few days. That's all she said." Olivia threw her hands in the air.

"Is she comin' back?" I began to panic. I couldn't catch my breath.

"Colt, I. Don't. Know. The note says she is, but I honestly don't know anything else."

I ran as fast as I could back to my truck. I couldn't think. I couldn't breathe. I just wanted to scream. What was I going to do if she didn't come back? I must have blacked out from the panic because I don't remember how I got to the beach. There was no one around. I went into the water until it was up to my neck. I couldn't hold it in any longer. I let out all my frustration and sadness in my screams until I had nothing left. I slowly dragged myself out of the water and drove home. I was exhausted in every way possible. The last thing I remember was praying *God, please help me* before falling onto my bed.

The next day, I just couldn't bring myself to do anything. I drudged through the motions of getting dressed. I went to the one place where I might find some guidance. I went to church.

I sat in a pew in the empty sanctuary about halfway up to the altar.

"God, I'm more confused than ever right now. I thought Callie was who You had for me. Was I wrong? I don't know if she left forever or if she's coming back. My heart is aching so much, God. It's almost more than I can bear. Please show me, God, what You want from me, what You have for me." Tears streamed down my face.

I finished my prayer. I wasn't sure how long I sat there in silence, but a peace washed over me. In that peace, God reminded me that He is in control. Things happen in His time, not mine. *Thank you, Lord.* I drove back to the ranch and did what I did every single day—I worked. I had to believe that God's will would work itself out. Whatever was to happen would happen. I just had to be patient and wait on Him. No matter how much it tore me up inside.

Chapter 36

Callie

When I got back to Edenton, I couldn't wait to see Colt to confess my feelings for him. I was finally ready. I was excited and nervous and everything in between. I just hoped and prayed he would be able to forgive me—for running away and for leaving without saying anything. I had trouble keeping to the speed limit. I needed to get to him. It was the day after I confronted my aunt. My head fought my heart over and over, but my heart finally won.

When I pulled up to the stable, the sky opened up and poured down on me. It was as if the rain was washing away every bad thing that had ever happened to me, washing the slate clean for a new beginning. I just hoped my new beginning was with Colt.

"Colt!" I raced through the door before I was completely soaked. My eyes darted in every direction, but he was nowhere to be found. My heart sank. I heard a snicker behind me, and when I turned around, my gaze was met by Warrior's soulful eyes. "Hey, boy," I said, moving to his stall and reaching out to pet him. "I'm sorry I haven't come to see you. Things are just . . . complicated right now. I've missed you." I kissed his nose.

"He's not the only one who's missed ya 'round here."

I turned to see who had spoken to me. "Oh, hey, Luke.

How are you?"

"I'm good. What're ya doin' here?" His face contorted into confusion.

"Long story, but I need to talk to Colt. Have you seen him?"

"No. Last I saw, he was in his truck, driving away."

"Okay. Thank you. I'll see you later. See you later, too, Warrior." I kissed the horse's nose once more before darting back out to my Jeep.

"*Now* what do I do?" I asked myself after settling into the driver's seat.

Maybe he's at home. If not, I'll just wait for him. As I approached Colt's house, his truck was gone, and no lights were on inside. I parked and made a mad dash for the cover of the porch. By then, I was completely drenched to the bone. I sat on the swing before noticing my ankle was throbbing. All I could do was wait. The rain had cooled the temperature to the point I began to shiver. Before long, the darkness overtook me, and I closed my eyes.

I was awakened by my name being called and a tingle on my arm. I blinked a few times, trying to focus on the silhouette before me. It was Colt's voice and his hand on my arm.

"Colt," I started as I opened my eyes.

"Hey. What're ya doin' here?" he asked with a perplexed expression.

"I . . . need . . . to . . . talk . . . to . . . you," I replied through chattering teeth.

"Well, let's get ya inside, in some dry clothes, and warmed up."

"Okay."

Colt pulled me up from the swing and helped me inside. "Why don't ya go take a warm shower, and I'll leave clothes outside the door."

"Thank you."

I closed the bathroom door. I made the mistake of glancing in the mirror. I was hideous with my hair a tangled, wet mess and mascara running down my face. I didn't stare too long before stepping into the shower. The water hit my body and enveloped me like a warm blanket. After my shower, I slipped into the clothes outside the door and put my hair up in a bun. I felt so much better, but that was the case anytime Colt was nearby. When I was halfway presentable, I searched the house for Colt. I walked into the kitchen and found him standing over a beautiful cake. It had white icing with coral-colored flowers. It was a one-layer cake, and Colt had lit one candle on top.

"Do ya know how hard it's been to keep the guys away from this thing?"

I giggled. "Colt, it's really beautiful. I can't believe you remembered my favorite color."

"Callie, I remember everything you've told me," he confessed, coming around the table. "Happy birthday, Callie . . . a day or two late." He smirked. "Now, make a wish."

My cheeks grew warm. I gazed up at him and smiled. I closed my eyes, made a wish, and blew out the candle.

"So, what did ya wish for?" Colt whispered.

"I can't tell you, or it won't come true," I whispered back. He pouted. "I'll let you know if it comes true. How about that?" I glanced at him.

"Okay." He stuck his bottom lip out further. "Do ya want a piece of cake?"

"Yeah, but can we talk first?" I really wanted to shove some cake into my mouth to calm my nerves. Food—my constant companion, my comforter. *No, Callie. You don't need to get lost in food anymore. You have people who genuinely*

173

love you here, especially a man. I swallowed hard.

"Sure."

I followed Colt into the living room and sat at the opposite end of the couch. I bent one leg underneath me and faced him. I didn't know where to begin, so I just started talking.

"I'm so sorry I ran the other day and left without saying anything. I ran because my aunt was in my head telling me all the things she has always said to me, like I'm not good enough, and no man will ever want me because I'm fat. I got scared that once you see my scars, you won't feel the same way . . ." I trailed off and peered over at him.

"Oh, Callie. Ya never gave me a chance." He sighed.

"I know. That's why I had to go away. I had to go back to Indianapolis and face my biggest demon. I had to go to my aunt's house and tell her I forgive her." I sighed and stared at my hands folded in my lap. "What I want to tell you more than anything, though," I paused to fill my lungs with enough air and courage, "is that I'm so in love with you, too."

Before I could get any other words out, Colt's lips were pressed to mine. It wasn't the desperate passion like the kiss on my birthday. It was soft, sweet, and loving—forgiving.

"So, does that mean you forgive me?" I gazed up at him through my lashes, hope filling my heart.

"There's nothing to forgive." Colt ran his thumb along my cheek before kissing me again. "Okay. We have to stop doing that. Not that I want to stop, but I also don't want to lose control. Do ya want some cake?" Colt rattled on as he ran his hand through his hair and down the back of his neck. He stood and peered down at me.

"Sure. I'd love some." I beamed at his retreating back. "But just a small one," I called after him. I put my fingers to my still-tingling lips and smiled even more. He still loved me.

He truly loved me. My heart began to sing. *Thank you, God. I know this was all You.*

"Thank you," I said as I took the plate Colt held out to me. I sliced my fork through the cake, stabbed it, and slid it into my mouth. I closed my eyes and moaned. "Oh my! Caitlyn and Marci sure know how to bake a cake. This is delicious!"

"That they do."

We stayed up most of the night talking, laughing, and snuggling.

"Thank you for the most wonderful birthday, Colt. P.S. my wish came true."

My head was on his chest. I glanced up at him when he didn't respond to find he had fallen asleep. I stayed snuggled next to him. I didn't want to wake him, but I also loved how it felt to be in his arms. For the first time in a long time, I allowed myself to truly think and dream about my future. I was excited about it. I couldn't wait to move back to the ranch and work with Colt and Warrior again. Hopefully, I could help with the Harvest Festival again, also. I sighed happily, closed my eyes, and allowed sleep to engulf me.

Chapter 37

Colt

I awoke to pain in my back and pressure on my side. I opened my eyes to find Callie fast asleep on my shoulder. So, it wasn't a dream. Callie was here, and she really did love me back. I heard commotion in the kitchen. I stood slowly, trying my best not to disturb her. I grinned at her sleeping face before tiptoeing into the kitchen to greet Richard.

"Mornin', Richard."

"Mornin', Colt. Sorry if I woke you up. I was trying my best to be quiet. So, what happened? Last you told me, she left town."

I shrugged. "That's what she left in a note to Olivia. When I got back to the house last night, though, she was soaked and sleeping on the porch. She told me she loves me, too." I flashed a wide, pearly smile.

"I don't remember seeing you smile like that since you were in high school. It's good to see it back on your face."

"Thanks. It feels good to have it there. It felt awesome waking up to her beside me, too. I think we are going to spend some time with Warrior today and go over things for the festival. I'm hoping she'll agree to move back into her cabin."

"It'll be good to have her back. She was missed for sure."

"Well, I'm gonna go get ready for the day. See ya in a bit

for breakfast."

"Take your time."

I let the shower's spray envelop me. I still couldn't believe Callie was in love with me, too. For the first time in a long time, my heart felt so full it might burst. I was looking forward to the future. "God, thank You for blessing me. I don't know what I did to deserve her, but I hope I never stop doing it." I prayed softly while turning off the water and grabbing my towel.

Chapter 38

Callie

"**M**orning, Richard."

"Mornin', Callie. So wonderful to see ya here. You've been missed."

"Aww. I've missed being here." I had a broad smile plastered to my face as I made my way around the island to give him a hug.

"I wanted to apologize for the misunderstanding."

"No need. It was completely my fault. My insecurities got the best of me," I confessed shyly. "I guess I should go freshen up."

"Okay. See you in a bit."

"Most definitely will. It smells so yummy in here."

I left the kitchen to search for Colt. I rounded the corner and almost plowed right into his chest. "Oh, hey there." My face warmed, and a shy smile spread across my lips.

"Hey." He grinned. "Good morning." He leaned down and kissed my cheek.

"Morning. Do you mind if I go home, shower, change my clothes, and come back over?"

"How about I'll pick you up at Olivia's, and we can go over to the café to meet with Marci and Caitlyn. Maybe we can get the Harvest Festival finalized today."

"That sounds perfect."

"Have ya thought about moving back into your cabin?" His face expressed eagerness.

"It's still empty?"

He stepped closer to me, lifted my chin so my eyes met his. "I told ya. You always have a place here . . . with me." He softly brushed his lips against mine.

"I could get used to those." I giggled.

"They're all yours for as long as ya want 'em."

Colt hugged me close. I could get used to those, too. I was amazed how safe, secure, and cared for I felt the instant his arms were around me. Every. Single. Time. I most definitely could get used to it.

"Okay. So, I'll see you in about an hour?" I glanced up at him.

"You can count on it." He led me out to my Jeep and opened my door for me.

"Thank you."

He responded by kissing my cheek and closing the door. "See ya later."

I drove back to Olivia's. I was on a cloud. I grinned bigger than I had in a long time, so much so, my cheeks were hurting.

"Olivia! I'm home!" I announced, barging through the door.

"Callie, where have you been?" She engulfed me in a hug.

"Sorry. Let's talk?"

We went into the living room.

"So, what is going on?" Olivia asked, sitting down facing me on the couch.

"I had to go back to Indianapolis to tell my aunt I forgive her."

"Wow."

"It was the only way I could get her out of my head, which was the only reason I ran from Colt when he told me he loved me. When I got back to town yesterday, I went straight to him. I fell asleep on the porch, drenched from the rain. Then, we talked most of the night before falling asleep on the couch." I laughed. "But not before I told him how I feel."

"And? What happened?" Olivia screeched.

"I mean, it was a little awkward this morning, but I'm sure it's just going to take a minute to go from friends to a relationship and no longer having to hide how we feel."

"I'm sure it will."

"He asked me if I'm going to move back into the cabin."

"Oh, really? Are ya?"

"I don't know. Do you think I should?"

"Yes! I mean, not that I don't love having ya here, but I saw how happy being at the ranch made ya. You deserve to be happy, Callie."

"I know. I did love being around all the horses, especially Warrior . . ." I sighed.

"And maybe a certain cowboy?"

"Yes." I giggled. "Okay. I'll come and get my stuff later. Colt is coming to pick me up to meet Marci and Caitlyn at the café so we can finalize the festival. Now, I have to get in the shower before Colt gets here." I jumped up off the couch. "And, Olivia, thank you."

"You're welcome. Love you."

"Love you."

I disappeared into the bathroom. My breath caught in my throat as I put my clothes on after drying off. I put on a cute dress. It was knee-length and pale pink. Turns out, I didn't mind dresses after all. I pulled my hair up in a ponytail. I applied a little mascara and lip gloss.

"It's just Colt." I blew out the breath that finally became dislodged. But I knew that wasn't true. Things *had* changed. We told each other how we felt. We were no longer *just* friends. "Just breathe." I inhaled deeply and then exhaled. "Okay. Here we go. God, this is in Your hands."

I walked into the living room to find Colt waiting for me. He glanced up, his eyes bulging. "You will never cease to take my breath away, Callie."

I bit my bottom lip. "What?"

Colt strode over to me, placed his hands on my cheeks, and softly stated, "You heard me."

Then, he kissed me. It was a whisper of a kiss, but it was amazing.

"We'd better get going," he whispered.

"Okay. After the meeting, can you help me with my stuff?"

"Ya mean you're moving back to the ranch?" His face lit up with excitement as he whisked me up off my feet in a hug. I giggled and held on tight.

"If you'll still have me."

"Always, Callie. Always."

"Okay. Put me down. We have to go." I giggled more.

"Okay. Okay."

"Olivia! I'll be back to get my stuff."

"No rush. See you later!"

Colt caught my hand and led me out the door. I couldn't get over how different I felt with him. It had only been hours since I confessed to him that I loved him, but it felt like ages ago. It wasn't a weird different like I thought it would be but a sweet different. A good different. I loved how he held my hand while we drove to the café and the sweet, soft kisses he had given me.

Chapter 39

Colt

When we arrived at the café and departed the truck, I took hold of Callie's hand and held on tight. It had taken me long enough to get her close to me. I wasn't about to let her go. I still couldn't believe the day before ended with Callie telling me she was in love with me, too. Ever since I woke up with her in my arms that morning, I couldn't wipe the grin from my face. I hadn't been that happy since before my dad passed.

The bells chimed, announcing we had arrived, and Caitlyn came out to greet us. "Hi, Uncle Colt." She catapulted into my arms in a hug.

"Hey, Caitlyn." I chuckled. "You must be feelin' better today."

"Much better. Thank you. Hi, Callie." Caitlyn greeted as she jumped back to the ground. Then, she gave Callie a hug.

"Hi. So glad to see you're feeling better. We missed you last week. By the way, thank you so much for the amazing birthday cake. It was absolutely beautiful and delicious."

"You're welcome. Mom and I had so much fun making it. It was hard to keep it a secret, though." She flashed a sheepish smile.

Callie bit her lip and whispered to Caitlyn, "I have trouble with secrets, too."

"Are you as excited as I am about the Harvest Festival?" Caitlyn asked with a squeal.

"Yes. I've never been to a festival, aside from the Fourth of July Festival, so I'm excited to see what goes into it but more so about attending."

"It's so much fun. Especially the dance the last night."

I watched their interaction. I loved that Callie fit so perfectly into my world. It was like she was always meant to be there. That just made me grin even more.

"Did I hear something about the Harvest Festival?" Marci asked, gliding into the dining area from the kitchen. She glanced down at our joined hands and squealed just like Caitlyn had moments before. "Does this mean you two finally told each other?" she asked, pointing to our hands.

"Yes," I replied.

A blush formed on Callie's cheeks, but heat flooded mine, too.

"Oh, this makes me so happy." Marci squealed again, giving us both a hug at the same time.

"Okay. Let's talk festival." Callie quickly changed the subject and clapped her hands with excitement.

"Yes, let's." Caitlyn nodded.

As I watched them, I couldn't believe the young, bubbly, beautiful blonde-haired girl that was Caitlyn was living the life she had. When she was in junior high, she was diagnosed with Juvenile Type I Diabetes and Epilepsy. I knew some days were a complete struggle for her, but she always had a smile for everyone and drew her strength from her faith in God. Caitlyn was the other reason I re-dedicated my life to Christ. I saw Jesus through her and just had to have it, too. A nudge came from my right side and brought me back to the present conversation.

"Sorry, what?"

"What do you think about having the dance in the barn this year? Just in case it rains." Callie peered over at me. How could I resist those eyes?

"Sure. That sounds great." I grinned.

A thought began to form in my mind. I would get to finish my dance with Callie that we started on her birthday. Then, another thought formed, and all I could do was grin more. Yes, this would be the best Harvest Festival yet. After a couple of hours, everyone agreed we were ready to begin setting up.

"I'll make sure the guys are ready to help with set up," I assured everyone. "The festival starts on the 21st and ends the 27th. That gives us just a little over two weeks to get everything ready to go."

"I think we should be able to do that," Marci stated with confidence. "Don't you think, Sis? We'll get your dad to help, too. Dyl will be at baseball camp until the last night. He's bummed he's going to miss it but excited about camp."

"Most definitely." Caitlyn agreed with a big toothy smile.

"Great! So, see ya tomorrow to start?" I asked.

"Yes," they both said in unison.

After we all exchanged hugs, I captured Callie's hand and led her out the door. When we reached the passenger side of my truck, I hauled her close and kissed her.

"What was that for?" Callie asked when I broke the kiss.

"I wanted one." I grinned guiltily.

"Not that I mind." She peered up at me. "Are you going to help me with my stuff today, or do we need to do it another day?"

"Definitely today. I like it better when you're at the ranch."

"Good. I like it better there, too, but don't tell Olivia." She giggled. Her laugh caused me to chuckle, too.

"Let's go." I opened the door so she could climb in.

Callie curtsied. "Well, thank you, kind sir."

"You're most welcome, my lady." I bowed.

After retrieving Callie's stuff from Olivia's and unloading it all at the cabin, we both flopped down on the couch.

"Do ya wanna come back to the house for supper, or ya can get unpacked if ya'd rather."

"I'll have dinner with everyone. It'll be great to see them, especially Luke." She smirked. I growled, which made her laugh. I drew her close. "Oh," she responded in surprise.

"You're all mine." I kissed her.

"And you are mine." She kissed me back.

When we broke apart, we both let out a hearty laugh. I had no idea what it was about Callie that made me feel so free, but I hoped it would always feel like that.

"We should probably get going." I stood and held out my hands to help Callie up.

"Do you mind if I drive myself, so I can just drive myself back? I'd like to spend some time with Warrior after dinner if that's okay."

"Callie, sweetheart, ya don't have to ask permission to do anything. You can do as ya please, just like everyone else. Besides, I know Warrior would love to spend time with ya also. He hasn't been the same since ya left. No one has." I peered down at her.

"Well, let's get going so we can eat and visit him."

I grabbed Callie's hand and walked her to her Jeep. Before she got in, I gave her a quick peck on the lips. I didn't understand why I felt the need to do that. But then again, I didn't understand a lot of things since her arrival here in Edenton. I had never been much for public displays of affection, but with Callie, I couldn't seem to help myself. Maybe it was because I had wanted to kiss her for so long but wasn't able to do so. I couldn't be sure. What I was sure of was that I wanted to keep doing it. Luckily, the Lord and His word helped me to know when to stop before temptation took over. It was a long, hard road but would be so worth it. More than anything, I wanted a relationship with Callie that was right in the eyes of God, and I would do everything in my power to protect that.

I had been so lost in thought I hadn't realized we had pulled up to the house. As we made our entrance into the kitchen, the guys began engulfing Callie in hugs to welcome her back.

"So, ya both finally decided to tell each other what everyone else already knew?" Luke chuckled as he sat down. "I'm surprised it took ya two this long to figure it out."

I glanced over to see Callie's "deer-in-headlights" expression.

"Well, ya know . . . we both have . . . stuff." I rubbed the back of my neck.

"Let's eat!" Austin called out.

Everyone sat down, and Richard gave thanks over the food.

"This is delicious, Richard. I have missed your cooking," Callie said after a few bites. "Don't tell Olivia." Her eyes darted around the table. That caused another round of laughter.

"Glad you like it. Also, so glad to have you back. Hopefully, for good this time?" He smiled as he glanced at her over his glasses. I could see the blood rush to Callie's cheeks. I still didn't know why I loved it so much.

"Ya ready to go?" I asked when the table was cleared and the dishes were washed, dried, and placed in the cabinets.

"Yes." She beamed up at me. "You don't have to go if you have something else you need to do."

"There's no place I'd rather be than with you." I berated myself for saying that, but it's how I felt.

"Okay. Let's go." She grinned.

I took Callie's hand and led the way to the stable. As soon as we breached the doorway, Warrior stomped and blew air through his nose to announce to us he was there.

"Hey, Warrior." Callie smiled at him. She placed a kiss on his nose. I loved watching them together, especially because Warrior was so different with Callie than anyone else. It was like they were kindred spirits. I could see God's hand in everything since Callie and Warrior arrived at the ranch. "Looks like we will be scar buddies forever." She grinned at Warrior.

"Can I see them?" I asked in an almost whisper.

"What?"

"Your scars. Can I see them?" I chewed my inner cheek, scared to see them, not because of how I'd feel about her, but because I didn't know if I could keep my anger in check.

"I . . . I guess," she stammered.

Callie turned around and lifted her shirt, inhaling a deep breath. I stared at her back and winced. How did she survive that? Never in my life have I wanted to hurt someone as badly as I wanted to hurt her aunt in that moment. But I couldn't think like that. Callie had forgiven her. God had forgiven her. I had to forgive her. Callie's scars matched Warrior's, except there were more of them on her. The rigid, raised scars covered almost every inch of her back. Scars covered scars. I reached out my hand, then immediately snatched it back. Hot tears stung my eyes.

"Oh, Callie."

She jerked her shirt down. "Did you get a good look and get your fill?" she asked coldly.

"Callie, don't do that." I sighed.

"Don't do what?"

"Don't shut me out."

She sighed deeply and turned to face me. "I'm sorry. I was just preparing myself."

"Preparing for what?"

Callie shrugged and stared at the ground. It dawned on me as I heard her voice in my head. *I was afraid once you see my scars, you won't feel the same way.*

"Callie, look at me." She kept her eyes on the ground. "Callie," I pleaded, placing my fingers under her chin to lift her face so her eyes met mine. "Look at me." I searched her eyes. "I'm not going anywhere."

"Promise?" Her lip trembled. Fear swirled in her eyes as the tears filled them to the brim.

"Oh, baby." I enveloped her in my arms. "I do."

Callie finally wrapped her arms around me. I would never get tired of having her in my arms. There would never be another for me. She had my heart. My whole heart.

"I love you so much, Callie," I whispered in her ear. She nuzzled closer. I raised her chin to kiss her again, making sure the love poured out of me and into her. "We should probably say goodnight." I sighed. If we were going to keep our relationship pure, she had to go back to her cabin, and I had to return to my house. No matter how much I hated it.

"I suppose we should. Sweet dreams, my handsome prince." Callie smirked and kissed my cheek. "I love you, too," she whispered before striding out of the stable.

I exhaled the minute she was out of sight.

Chapter 40

Callie

The next two weeks flew by as everyone worked together to transform the ranch into a fall wonderland. There were so many booths: face painting, pumpkin carving, baked goods from neighboring farms. Marci and Caitlyn had a booth for the café and bakery. Olivia displayed her artwork. Marie and Carl had a booth displaying Marie's baked goods and Carl's hand-made wood plaques and animals, to name a few. Some of the guys even gave horse rides. There was a corn maze and hayrides as well. Everyone seemed to be enjoying their time there. It made me happy to see people laughing and having a good time. That is what life was truly about—laughing and spending time with family and friends.

When the last night of the festival finally arrived, excitement for the dance was in the air. I had been so excited to experience each day of the festival and what it held. I was like a child in all my wonder at everything the festival had to offer. Each day was completely magical. Ever since I found forgiveness for my aunt, life seemed to take on a whole new meaning. I saw things in a different light, as a child experiences things for the first time. I was most excited about the dance. I couldn't wait for Colt to see me in my dress and to dance and be close.

Marci and Caitlyn had gone shopping with me. I felt so beautiful when I looked in the mirror. The hard part had been not telling or showing Colt. He had asked more than once. I finally caved and told him the color. I couldn't wait to wear it for him. It was an off-the-shoulder, knee-length, yellow, pleated dress. I planned to pair it with my cowgirl boots that were brown and embroidered with sunflowers.

As I waited for Colt, I saw he was talking with Chuck. They were deep in conversation and appeared to be studying something in Colt's hand. I strode over to them anyway. As I got closer, I heard the tail end of their conversation.

"So, will ya help me out?" Colt asked Chuck.

"Of course. Whatever ya need me to do."

"Hi, guys. Whatcha talking about?" I interrupted.

"Oh . . . Chuck is going to help me with a little project I have coming up. No big deal," Colt replied as he stuffed whatever was in his hand in his pocket.

I wanted so badly to know what they were talking about and what Colt had just shoved in his pocket. I raised a brow but then shrugged it off. If Colt wanted me to know, he would tell me. I'd press him later when no one was around. I bet I could get him to tell me.

"So, are ya excited about the dance tonight, Callie?" Chuck asked, changing the subject.

"Yes, I am."

"Ya got a hot date?" Chuck laughed.

"As a matter of fact, I do. With the most gorgeous man on the planet," I confessed, winking at Colt. I turned to him and wrapped my arms around his neck.

"Well, I'll leave you two and go find my wife and daughter."

"Bye, Chuck," we said at the same time.

"So, ya have a hot date, do ya?"

"I sure do." I stood on my tiptoes and gave him a peck on the lips.

"Oooooh," I heard from behind Colt.

We turned to see Marci with a big grin on her face. Colt and I let out hearty laughs.

"Hey, Marci. How's the booth doing?" I asked.

"Great! It seems all the booths are doing really well."

"That makes me so happy." I giggled with delight. Marci, Chuck, Caitlyn, and I spent a good part of the day getting the barn ready for the dance, and I couldn't wait for Colt's reaction. "Marci, I just wanted to say again how much I appreciate your, Chuck's, and Caitlyn's help with everything." I gave her a hug.

"It was a pleasure. We had so much fun. I can't wait to see you in your dress tonight." Colt groaned behind me. Marci and I laughed. "I've gotta get back to Sis and the booth. I'll see you both later."

Marci waved before retreating to her booth. Colt and I walked around hand-in-hand for only the second time that week. We had hoped to spend more time together, but the week was busier than expected. The glances and smiles we received made me feel as if my cheeks would be permanently red.

"Well, it's almost time for the dance. I guess we should go and get ready," I suggested.

Colt stopped to glance at me. I grinned up at him. He moved closer and softly said, "I can't wait to see you in your dress." His warm breath lingered on my skin, the softness of his words sending goosebumps surging down my neck, all the way to my toes. He kissed my cheek before letting go of my hand and strutting away. I shook my head and giggled.

I began to trek back to my cabin. My ankle was still sore at times, but it was getting better, and my limp wasn't quite as severe. As I made my way back to my cabin, I thought about the town and the people in it. I had fallen in love with it and all of the people I had met. I couldn't imagine living anywhere else. It truly was a magical place that had breathed new life into me.

After slipping into my dress and making my best attempt to tame my wild hair, I strode into the barn and was transported back to my birthday with the twinkle lights everywhere. The only differences were the whole town was there and a live band. Even though I had helped decorate, it still captivated me. It was romantic and festive all at the same time.

"It looks almost like it did on your birthday except livelier," Colt observed from behind me before kissing my cheek. "Y'all did an amazin' job."

I clasped his hand, taking in the musky scent of his cologne. "Thank you."

I scanned the room. I saw Caitlyn talking to Wyatt. She looked stunning in her red cap-sleeve, off-the-shoulder flare dress paired with her cream-colored, snakeskin ankle boots. Her long blonde hair was scooped up off her neck and curled at the ends. She was surely a gorgeous sight. She had become such a good friend over the time I had been there and was a true inspiration with how she chose to deal with her health issues. She didn't talk about her faith much, but anyone who met her could see Jesus reflected in her. My life shined brighter because she was in it.

Not too far from her were Marci and Chuck. Marci wore an elegant, navy-blue, V-neck, sleeveless, knee-length dress. She was a vision of beauty, just like her daughter. Chuck was handsome in his dark gray suit, navy-blue tie, and jeans. They were talking to Dylan. He had just returned from baseball camp hosted by the minor league team there in Edenton. He fidgeted with his tie, loosening it and unbuttoning the top button of his shirt. I chuckled. No way he picked that outfit on his own. Marci must have made him wear the tie and ironed shirt. He caught my gaze, and I nodded, giving him a thumbs up. He snatched the end of his tie and held it up, sticking his tongue out as if it was choking him—typical teenage boy.

I was so blessed by the friendships I had made, but none more important than Olivia, my very first best friend. "Cal, you look so beautiful," Olivia screeched as she hugged me.

"So do you," I responded, taking in Olivia in her olive-green skater dress.

Jon appeared behind Olivia, obviously enjoying his view of her. He raised his brows up and down and fanned himself, sticking his tongue out as if he was about to overheat. I did my best to stifle the giggle bubbling inside me. Olivia's eyes narrowed, and she whipped around, almost colliding with Jon. He planted a loud smooch on her cheek. Olivia's mouth moved into the shape of an "O" in surprise. Jon lifted her in the air and whisked her away to the dance floor. I burst out laughing as Jon broke out into 70s John Travolta moves to a country song, no less. My eyes finally made it to the man standing next to me. I wasn't sure I'd ever get used to just how handsome Colt was. I surveyed him from head to toe and back up again. I focused on his tie.

"How did you get a tie that shade of yellow?" My brow furrowed.

Colt's cheeks became rosy. I raised a brow. So, he *did* get embarrassed. Nice to see *him* blush for a change. "I asked Marci to pick it out for me since she knew the color of your dress."

"Oh." I poked my tongue into my cheek. "So, you're a

cheater, cheater, pumpkin eater." I giggled.

Colt clutched his hand over his heart. "Aww. Ya caught me. Please forgive me."

I gazed up at him. "I suppose I could do that."

He leaned down and whispered in my ear, "Ya do look absolutely gorgeous in that dress." His breath on my ear made goosebumps pop up along my arms. I looked into his eyes and could tell he meant every word. I smiled and gave him a soft, sweet kiss on the lips.

"You are looking quite handsome yourself. Told you I had a hot date." I smirked. A slow song began to play, and I recognized it as the song from my birthday. "Did you plan this?"

Colt shrugged and grinned like a little schoolboy caught with his hand in the cookie jar. "May I have this dance?" He extended his hand.

"Yes, you may." I took his hand and curtsied. He wrapped his arms around my waist, and I clasped mine around his neck, the electricity flowing through us so strong, I didn't think I'd be able to hang on much longer.

About halfway through the song, Chuck tapped Colt's shoulder. "May I cut in?"

"Only for a little bit."

Chuck twirled me around so fast, it made me lightheaded, and I giggled. "Are ya having a good time?" he asked.

"The best," I laughed, still feeling a little dizzy.

"Well, it's about to get better. Turn around."

"What? Why?"

What was happening? My breath caught in my throat. My palms started to sweat as I slowly turned around, noticing all eyes were on me. Heat burned my cheeks. I hated being the center of attention—especially when I had no idea what was going on. My heart was pounding so hard. I was afraid it would burst.

"What's going on?" I asked no one in particular. Time stood still. When I finally turned all the way around, Colt was kneeling with a ring box in his hand. I gasped as I raised my fingertips to my lips and tears began to pool. "Colt, what are you doing?"

"Callie, I think I may have fallen for ya the minute ya breezed into the Bistro your first full day here. I truly believe God blessed the broken road that led me to you. You've become my best friend, and I can't imagine my future without ya in it. Callie St. Claire, will you bless me by bein' my wife?"

I was speechless. My tongue was glued to the top of my mouth, dry as cotton, screaming for water. What was happening? Was he really proposing? I couldn't believe it. I was so overwhelmed with emotion. I could feel my heart beating wildly throughout my entire body. I wanted to scream yes with my entire being, but the words wouldn't come out of my mouth. I looked down at the open red velvet box. Nestled inside was a silver Claddagh ring. He really did listen and remember. I had mentioned the ring at the Fourth of July Festival.

"Say yes!" Caitlyn shouted.

A round of giggles and chuckles filled the space encircling us. Everyone went quiet, waiting for me to answer. It was so quiet I could hear a pin drop.

"I'm sorry." I raised my hand to my chest and swallowed hard. "I couldn't find my voice for a minute. Colton Andrews, I will marry you on one condition."

"Of course, you would have a condition." He laughed. "What is it?"

"Only if you bless me right back."

"I can definitely do that," he responded as he smiled and

stood. He slid the ring on my finger and gathered me in his arms while the whole town cheered.

Epilogue

Colt

It was one year later and once again the last night of the Harvest Festival. However, instead of a dance, there was a wedding—*our* wedding. I couldn't believe Callie agreed to marry me exactly one year ago. I had been so used to losing people who were important to me. Although I *almost* lost her, God brought us together. It hadn't been an easy year for either of us, missing parents and keeping God at the center of our relationship, but we made it through. Soon, Callie would be my wife. Soon, I would be her husband.

As I stood at the altar with the pastor, I said a silent prayer. *Thank you, Lord, for blessing me far more than I deserve. I promise to honor You in all we do. Amen.*

I wished my dad was there to stand with me. My heart was racing, and my hands became clammy as I waited for my beautiful bride to come down the aisle to meet me in holy matrimony. I hoped to see her eyes sparkle, for the first time, because of me.

* * *

Callie

I had asked Caitlyn, Marci, and Olivia to be my bridesmaids and asked if Carl would walk me down the aisle. I was so happy when they all agreed. The girls fussed over me, working my hair into a curly updo and putting on what felt like a pound of makeup. When it was time, I stepped into my white dress. It fell just above my knees. I was going to wear my boots but opted to go barefoot and paint my toes coral to match my bouquet and the bridesmaids' dresses. They were supposed to wear boots also but chose to match me, except their toes were painted a cream color.

"It's time." Carl knocked on the door to announce his presence. "Oh, Callie, you look breathtaking."

"You really think so?" I ran my hands down my dress.

"I know so. Colt is a lucky, lucky man."

"Thank you and thank you, again, for standing in for my dad." I kissed his cheek.

I swiped a tear that threatened to fall. That had been the hardest part of the last year—planning my wedding without my parents. I knew it had been just as hard for Colt not having his dad to stand at the altar with him, but we had the most amazing friends who had become family. I still couldn't believe Colt asked me to marry him one year ago. I finally found a man who loved everything about me.

"Shall we?" Carl asked, offering his arm.

"Yes." I rubbed my hands down my sides to try to get them to stop shaking.

I watched as Olivia, Marci, and Caitlyn glided down the aisle with Jon, Chuck, and Wyatt. Then, it was my turn. My heart pounded loudly. I took a deep breath and exhaled.

Carl whispered, "You ready?"

"More than I have ever been in my life," I whispered back.

As Carl guided me down the aisle, I glanced at all those who were standing on either side. Those people had become my family. A family I didn't even know I longed for until I found them. And then, there was the man standing at the end of the aisle waiting for me. He was so much more than any man I had ever dreamt up in my mind. Yes, God had a plan when He sent me on my journey to Edenton. He had, indeed, blessed the broken road that led me straight to Colt.

Available Soon . . .

FINDING REDEMPTION RANCH
(*Edenton Bay Romance* Series, Book 2)

BY ELIZABETH WOODROW

Dear reader:

Thank you for your interest in and purchase of *Mending Broken Roads (Edenton Bay Romance Series, Book 1)*. If you enjoyed this book, please be sure to obtain a copy of *Finding Redemption Ranch (Edenton Bay Romance Series, Book 2)*, available soon at major book retailers.

Sincerely,

Van Rye Publishing, LLC

From the Publisher

Thank You from the Publisher

Van Rye Publishing, LLC ("VRP") sincerely thanks you for your interest in and purchase of this book.

VRP hopes you will please consider taking a moment to help other readers like you by leaving a rating or review of this book at your favorite online book retailer. Depending on the retailer, you can do so by flipping past the last page of your e-book (to the rating and review page) or by visiting the book's product page (and locating the button for leaving a rating or review).

Thank you!

Resources from the Publisher

Van Rye Publishing, LLC ("VRP") offers the following resources to readers and to writers.

For *readers* who enjoyed this book or found it useful, please consider receiving updates from VRP about new and discounted books like this one. You can do so by following VRP on Facebook (at www.facebook.com/vanryepub) or Twitter (at www.twitter.com/vanryepub).

For *writers* who enjoyed this book or found it useful, please consider having VRP edit, format, or fully publish your own book manuscript. You can find out more and submit your manuscript at VRP's website (at www.vanryepublishing.com).

Thank you again!

Acknowledgments

G od, first and foremost, thank you for giving me the ability to tell this story. Thank you for your never-ending love, mercy, forgiveness, and grace. May we never take it for granted. **Steven Malichi, Jr.**, we spent many school days chatting about our writings. When you published your children's book, it inspired me to pick up my paper and pen again. I am forever grateful. **Matt Turner**, you encouraged me from the beginning to keep writing the story. You never stopped believing this book would get published. Your support and encouragement will be with me always. **Keith Hildebrand**, without your proofing and suggestions, this book would be far less than it is today. Thank you for your friendship and willingness to read this story over and over and over again. **Ania Ray**, we have become fast internet friends. Your words of encouragement were never wasted. I appreciate you more than you know. **Rebecca Carpenter**, you offered to edit my book, and I will never forget that. My book would not be what it is without your guidance and advice. Thank you so much! **Van Rye Publishing**, I cannot thank you enough for taking a chance on this writer. I will always be grateful! Finally, **Marci, Chuck, Dylan, and Caitlyn**, thank you for allowing me to make you a part of my story. I hope I have written something you can be proud to be a part of, and I hope that your girl lives on through my stories in a way that brings you peace and happiness. Your friendship means the world to me.

About the Author

ELIZABETH WOODROW was raised in a small town in eastern Indiana called Connersville. Faith and family are considered most important to Elizabeth and are reflected in her writing. Elizabeth holds a Bachelor of Science degree in Criminal Justice and a Master of Public Administration degree, both from Indiana Wesleyan University. She currently resides in Indianapolis, Indiana with her Chihuahua/Dachshund dog, Payslee and her Tortoiseshell Calico cat, Princess.